# MRS. POLLIFAX
## and the
# HONG KONG BUDDHA

# MRS. POLLIFAX
## AND THE
# HONG KONG BUDDHA

•

## Dorothy Gilman

**THORNDIKE PRESS • THORNDIKE, MAINE**

**Library of Congress Cataloging in Publication Data:**

Gilman, Dorothy, 1923-
  Mrs. Pollifax and the Hong Kong Buddha.

  1. Large type books.  I. Title.
[PS3557.I433M68  1986]     813'.54  ✱  86-1353
ISBN 0-89621-708-6 (alk. paper)

Large Print edition available through arrangement with
Doubleday and Company, Inc.

Large Print edition available in the British Commonwealth
through arrangement with Robert Hale.

Cover design by Armen Kojoyian.

# 1

It was raining – a driving spring rain that slashed at the windows – and Mrs. Pollifax hoped that it was not raining in the wilds of Vermont, where Cyrus had gone for a ten-day bird-watching expedition that would find him crouching for hours in the shrubbery or ensconced in a tree with field glasses. She had remained behind – quite wisely, she thought now – to deal with the carpenters swarming over the old house they'd bought, and to which they were adding a greenhouse for her geraniums, a bird-watching balcony for Cyrus and a bay window that was to be placed slightly off-center, a decision that deeply pained Mr. Lupalak, the contractor, a man who liked to dot every *i* and cross every *t*. Indeed from the part in the exact center of his dark hair it was plain that symmetry was a passion with him; Mr. Lupalak was a man to be watched.

Standing at the window and staring out at the very green, very wet landscape, Mrs. Pollifax wondered for the first time if she were really going to *like* the country. She could admire the sweep of green lawn — wet; the curve of road beyond — empty; the spire of a church barely visible above a dripping willow tree; but it was certainly a scene that lacked movement, sound and drama. When the carpenters left — they were making a great deal of noise in the basement this morning, cutting beams for the balcony — she wondered if it were not going to seem, perhaps, a trifle...unoccupied? She knew that out there in the grass and among the hollows there was a teeming wildlife — mice, toads, ants and there were rumors of a hedgehog behind the stone wall — but what the scene plainly lacked, she thought, was *people*.

Mrs. Pollifax enjoyed people: of all shapes, sizes, types and temperaments.

And then quite suddenly, as if the fates had eavesdropped, there was movement in that placid landscape as a car drove down Route 2, stopped, backed, turned and raced up the driveway toward her, sending plumes of water into the air as it hurtled through puddles to come to a stop near her front door.

"Now who...?" murmured Mrs. Pollifax.

From the car emerged a very pleasant-looking young man wearing a boisterous glen-plaid suit and matching vest, and carrying an attaché case: a man very familiar and dear to her who reminded her at once that her past included not only the growing of prize-winning geraniums but a great deal of drama, excitement, danger and people.

She had opened the door to him even before he reached it. "Bishop!" she cried. "What a surprise! How on earth—!"

"Devil of a time finding you," he said, giving her an exuberant hug. "I hear the sound of buzz saws from somewhere — are they building you an ark?"

She laughed. "It doesn't always rain in the country and if you'd only called first I could have given you terribly efficient directions. I'll put on some coffee. Oh, it's good to see you, come and look at our house."

"Love to," he said. "Where's Cyrus?"

"He left three days ago; he's in Vermont."

"Uh-oh," said Bishop.

Mrs. Pollifax gave him a quick, attentive glance. *Not* a social call, she thought, and felt a curious little stirring of anticipation and excitement. "Now *that's* a strange reaction," she told him.

He ignored this. "Put the coffee on and show me around — unless you charge for a guided

tour. I've not much time," he added paren-
thetically as he dropped his attaché case on the
pink-and-red flowered couch.

Mrs. Pollifax led him from room to room:
upstairs to the three gabled bedrooms, two of
them with fireplaces; downstairs through the
kitchen into the dining room with its flagstoned terrace just beyond, and then into the
greenhouse, which as yet lacked glass. She
took him into the basement and introduced
him to Mr. Lupalak, who regarded Bishop's
plaid suit with something approaching awe,
and to everything Bishop responded with
exactly the right words, but Mrs. Pollifax felt
that his mind was elsewhere, and she wondered.

They arrived back in the dining room at last,
where Mrs. Pollifax poured coffee for them
both, brought out napkins, sugar, a plate of
macaroons, and sat down to face him across
the polished trestle table. Behind Bishop the
wind and rain attacked the sliding glass doors,
the flagstoned terrace glistened wetly and one
lone forsythia bush struggled bravely to brighten
the scene with color.

"And how is Carstairs?" inquired Mrs. Pollifax, nibbling on a macaroon.

"Fine," said Bishop. "Considering the seden-
tary life he leads, full of stress and tension,

I regard him as a medical phenomenon. He resists running, jogging and even walking, and in effect defies every known law of health. And how is Cyrus?" he asked with equal politeness.

"Bird-watching."

He nodded. "And you're still Mrs. *Reed-Pollifax*?"

"Defying every known law of convention, yes," she responded. "Cyrus insisted."

An interesting silence fell between them as Bishop eyed her speculatively and she in turn waited patiently. "All right, Bishop," she said at last, smiling. "You can't possibly expect me to believe that you just happened to be in the neighborhood."

"No," he said, eating his third macaroon.

"No *what?*"

He swallowed. "No I didn't happen to be in the neighborhood," he admitted cheerfully. "I needed a plane, a taxi, a limousine and a rented car to reach you. Except I'd expected Cyrus to be here."

"He isn't," she pointed out.

"No, but we thought this time, now that you're married and all — however, it can't be helped. The thing is," he said, "we need you. Need you badly, and at once."

"For what?" she asked, "and what does 'at once' mean?"

11

He put down his cup of coffee. "If you can help us," he said quietly, "it means now. No time to call or collect Cyrus, no time for anything. You'd leave with me now, within the hour." With a glance at his watch he added, "By twelve noon."

Mrs. Pollifax glanced at her own watch: it was exactly five minutes after eleven. "Bishop! And you took fifteen minutes to tour the house!"

He smiled sheepishly. "I had some thinking to do — reassessing — and damn it I can't help my having been brought up to be polite and all that sort of thing — and we did expect Cyrus to be here, but his absence doesn't change our needing you. Actually rather desperately," he admitted.

Of course it was quite impossible, she told herself, she was too involved — and there was the bay window, and Cyrus not knowing — "Why me?" she asked. "And where?"

"Hong Kong," said Bishop.

*Hong Kong*...the sun shone in Hong Kong, she remembered. Brilliantly.

"You remember Sheng Ti?" asked Bishop.

She did indeed remember Sheng Ti. Not many months ago she had sat under a culvert with him in a Chinese town called Turfan, and after hearing how he was *hai fen*, or a "black person" in China, living without papers or home or identity, she had persuaded her co-agent to smuggle him out of China along with the man named Wang Shen whom they'd been sent into the country to rescue.

She nodded. "Of course I remember Sheng Ti – a very intelligent young man, his talents absolutely wasted as an outcast, or hooligan, as they call it."

"You're aware that he's in Hong Kong?"

"You told me so at our wedding. It sounded," she added tartly, "as if you didn't know what else to do with him and he was simply *dumped* there."

Bishop said dryly, "Well, no one had anticipated your largesse, you know; we'd expected two men to come over the mountains and through Kashmir, not three. Except he wasn't exactly dumped in Hong Kong, as you phrase it – you do us a disservice there – he was *placed* there. With one of our agents."

"Oh!" she said.

"Yes, and to put it in a nutshell, my dear Mrs. Pollifax – because the hands on that clock behind you are relentlessly in motion – we are growing very *very* worried about that agent, and your friend – your *friend* Sheng Ti – is the only person in a position to give us some clues."

"What would he know?" she said doubtfully.

"He works for the man, he's on the premises, we know that much from our Hong Kong contacts. The agent's name is Detwiler, he's a Eurasian, his cover a business called Feng Imports, Ltd., a small business importing diamonds and gems of all kinds. Old Feng runs the shop, Detwiler handles the importing, and Sheng Ti is one of two employees in the shop."

"And you're worried about Detwiler...?"

"I can't tell you how worried," said Bishop. "The man knows too much, he has a lot to offer. He went too far in his last report, the information he sent the department so patently false that we went back over previous ones and discovered that beginning about two months ago he's been feeding us doctored information. In a word, something's up, he's double-crossing us, and we suspect he's into something self-serving, nefarious and quite detrimental to our interests. Certainly he's no good to us anymore and we have every intention of finding out why, who he's working for now, what information he's been selling elsewhere and what the hell's going on. What's more," he added, "someone's put the fear of God — or Satan, perhaps — into your friend Sheng Ti."

Startled, she said, "How do you know that?"

He countered with, "Why do you think it's you we need so urgently? Because we sent two people into Feng Imports to try and approach Sheng Ti — you know, friendly conversation, the suggestion of a beer after work, a movie, a girl — no dice, the verdict was 'This is a guy who's terrified and in a panic.' Which, I might add, only confirms our suspicions of something *very* wrong at Feng Imports."

"And you feel that Sheng Ti might talk to me," said Mrs. Pollifax.

Bishop nodded. "He knows you. After all, it was thanks to you that he was smuggled out of Turfan and China; he trusts you, you're a familiar face." He stopped and glanced at his watch again. "There's more to this, of course, but that's the rough sketch of the situation. You're the only person who can get through to Sheng Ti, and we need what he can give us. We *must* know what's going on at Feng Imports."

"Yes," said Mrs. Pollifax.

Bishop looked at her and said gravely, "It could, of course, be dangerous — there's that, too — if you can't find Sheng Ti and have to sniff around Feng Imports."

Mrs. Pollifax nodded, considered his words for a moment and then stood up and carried the pot of coffee into the kitchen. "It's just eleven twenty-five," she told Bishop. "If you'll rinse out these cups and empty the coffee grounds —"

15

"You'll go!" cried Bishop joyously.

She turned, smiling at him. "It isn't raining in Hong Kong, is it? Yes I'll go, and now, if you'll excuse me—" She hurried upstairs, snatched her suitcase from the closet and crammed into it slacks, skirt and blouses, toothbrush, walking shoes and pajamas. Into her purse she tucked her passport, quickly changed into a purple wool suit, chose a pink shirt and placed on her head a hat that was a garden of brilliant red and pink roses. She then sat down at the desk and reached for a pen to write Cyrus a hasty note. *There's no way to reach you,* she wrote, *this is all terribly unexpected. Bishop is here — he hoped you could be, too — I'm off to Hong Kong in fifteen minutes, will phone, or you phone, I'll be...* "Bishop," she called, "where will I be staying and for how long?"

"Give it a week," Bishop shouted back, "and we've booked you in the Hong Kong Hilton."

*...at the Hong Kong Hilton, back in a week, don't forget how dear you are, love love love Emily.*

She read it over and added *P.S. DO not allow Mr. Lupalak to center bay window!* and then for just a moment she allowed herself to contemplate Cyrus's reaction when he found her gone and read the note. She had promised never again to work for Carstairs without Cyrus going with her; on the other hand Cyrus had in-

16

sisted that she never forfeit another assignment because of him.

"Won't have you caged, m'dear," he'd said. "Waited too damn many years for someone as full of surprises as you are. Don't want to change anything about you."

Dear Cyrus, she thought, how fortunate she'd been to meet him in Zambia, where he had been traveling with his daughter, Lisa, and where she had been looking for an assassin. Cyrus had saved her life, and then she had saved his, which at once provided grounds for a warm friendship, except that from the beginning Cyrus had made it clear that he had much more than friendship in mind.

This thought was interrupted by Bishop's words *it could be dangerous — there's that, too,* and she nodded: yes there was always that. Finding and talking with Sheng Ti sounded a relatively small assignment but so had her trip to mainland China a year ago, except that no one had expected the KGB to be involved, nor had Carstairs envisioned murder, a runaway horse, a broken wrist or the long hours of interrogation she'd undergone by the Chinese Security Police. Still, it had all ended well, she reminded herself cheerfully; her wrist had mended nicely, Wang Shen had been smuggled safely across the mountains and out of that adventure had come the realization that Cyrus Reed was absolutely vital to her future and not to be put off any longer.

And now she had been married to Cyrus for ten months and she smiled as she looked around a room that was filled with a sense of his presence. She could only hope that he would understand that she was needed.

"I'm *needed,*" she said aloud, and resolutely folded the note and moved to lock her suitcase.

It was ten minutes to the hour when she carried her note and suitcase down the stairs, and seeing her, Bishop whistled.

"Do you water those roses every night? What a hat," he marveled. "What a *hat!*"

"Thank you," she said demurely, and proceeded down into the basement to explain to an astonished Mr. Lupalak that she was leaving and would not be back that afternoon, or for quite a few afternoons, that he must tell Mr. Reed there was a note for him in the usual place, and would he please not fail her about the bay window, it was to be *slightly off-center.* She returned to Bishop sighing. "I'm sure he thinks I'm leaving Cyrus," she said. "For that matter I don't believe anyone in the neighborhood believes that we're married, what with me being Mrs. Reed-Pollifax."

Bishop grinned. "I could whip down and tell

him I was at your wedding."

Mrs. Pollifax gave him a mischievous smile. "No — everyone needs a bit of mystery in their lives, don't you think? Let Mr. Lupalak believe what he likes." With this she tucked the note for Cyrus in the refrigerator, removed her raincoat from the coat closet and at precisely twelve noon walked out into the rain to the car with Bishop, thoroughly prepared now for Hong Kong and wondering what it might hold for her in the way of adventure.

# 2

# MONDAY

Boarding the plane in San Francisco for the second leg of her trip, Mrs. Pollifax found herself astonished once again by the hordes of people hurrying from point A to point B – or C or D – with such enormous fixity of purpose; a world one forgot, she remembered, as soon as one triumphantly arrived. She tried to think of a similar world outside and beyond ordinary life, urgent and capsulated and shed like a skin once left behind. Perhaps a hospital, she mused, where people also shared a great fixity of purpose and where they also, she thought wryly, moved from point A to point B – or C or D – experiencing a life totally removed from the outside world...

"Oh – I beg your pardon!" she said, treading

on the heel of the man in front of her. He turned and gave her a chilling look; refusing intimidation, she said pointedly, "You *did* stop very suddenly."

The man's glance was like an assault, rendering her a mere object that had affronted him. Tall, thin, immaculately dressed, a lean and hungry face with pockmarked cheeks and cold eyes – *not* a pleasant young man she decided as he turned into seat 21-A and she proceeded down the aisle to 48-B, relieved to see that 48-A was already occupied, and by a far more pleasant-looking gentleman.

The plane took off, banking over a sapphire blue harbor to head into the setting sun, and presently her seat companion turned to her and said, "Would you care to see my copy of *Newsweek?*"

By the second hour they had exchanged names – his was Albert Hitchens – and shortly after dinner they settled down to a long talk about psychic phenomena, for Mr. Hitchens, it turned out, was a psychic.

"It's my dharma," he said simply.

He was not a prepossessing man; he was scarcely taller than her own five feet five; his complexion was swarthy, his features nondescript and for a man in his forties his clothes were casual in the extreme – he was wearing faded jeans, a knit shirt and sneakers – but his eyes were penetrating and a very curious silver in color, which the darkness of his skin accentuated and turned almost translucent.

Mrs. Pollifax, adept at karate, experienced in Yoga and very familiar with Zen, merely nodded at the word dharma. "Although," she admitted, "I do have trouble with the differences between karma and dharma."

"Ah yes," he said, nodding. "Dharma, you know, is the essence of one's individual existence – one's *work*, you might say – whereas karma, of course, is the force generated from past lives that determines our destiny in this one."

The slightly pedantic tone apparently came from the many lectures he gave; he was, to her surprise, a professional psychic, having written several books about it and having taught courses at colleges in the Boston area and having done considerable work for the Boston police in finding missing persons.

"Which," he explained, three hours into their flight, "is why I'm going to Hong Kong. One of my former students at Boston University, a delightful young man of Chinese origin, cabled and telephoned from Hong Kong several days ago pleading for help in finding a missing relative of his."

"And do you think you can?" Mrs. Pollifax asked with interest.

He said firmly, "There will be *something.*"

Mrs. Pollifax, glancing into his face, conceded that he was probably right because there was certainly something very unusual, almost otherworldly, about Mr. Hitchens's eyes. "But how do you do it?" she asked. "I've only once met someone with such a gift — a gypsy — and there wasn't time to ask. How do you begin? What happens?"

"It's a matter of impressions," he explained. "I can hold an object belonging to the missing person and it will tell me whether he's alive or dead...Or sometimes I go into trance, perhaps, and receive impressions — pictures, actually — of where he can be found."

"Impressions," she murmured, and as a movement down the aisle caught her glance she said, "Tell me your impression of that man, the one returning from the men's room." It was the man on whose heel she'd stepped.

Mr. Hitchens obligingly followed her glance, narrowing his eyes. "Now that," he said distastefully, "is as black an aura as I've seen for a long time." He shook his head. "A great deal of violence surrounds that man."

"Inside or outside?" asked Mrs. Pollifax curiously.

"If a man is a killer of life," said Mr. Hitchens with even more distaste, "does it matter how?"

Mrs. Pollifax smiled. "No, I don't suppose it does. Actually I happened to walk down the aisle behind him and bump into him and his eyes tried to kill — no, *annihilate* me," she told him.

Mr. Hitchens nodded. "A word whose root is *nihil*, meaning to reduce to nothing, to destroy. But tell me more of the gypsy you met, it interests me."

Mrs. Pollifax at once told him about Anyeta Inglescu, a queen of gypsies, and they then settled down to an enthusiastic discussion of out-of-body experiences, faith healing, precognition, energy and predestination, during which — surprisingly — she learned that he, too, was to stay at the Hilton Hong Kong.

"Perhaps we could breakfast together when we reach the hotel," he suggested.

"You're not being met by your friend?" she said, startled.

"I chose not to be," he said. "I want first to gather impressions—"

"That word again," said Mrs. Pollifax, smiling.

"—rest for several hours, meditate and clear my head. My young friend is to call for me at noon, we'll lunch and then get to work. But I find your vibrations quite energizing and not at all distracting," he told her, smiling for the first time since they'd met. "Unless of course you have other plans?"

Mrs. Pollifax assured him that she had no other plans and that she would be delighted to have breakfast with him at the hotel, and following this they each fell into naps, sleeping through a perpetual dawn and several time zones, until some hours later, reeling with jet lag, they walked off the plane at Kai Tak Airport in Hong Kong.

At Passport Control the man with the violent aura stood in line ahead of Mrs. Pollifax and she saw that it was a Canadian passport that he offered to the officer; at the luggage carousel he went off with only one very expensive-looking pigskin overnight bag. After that she lost interest in him, and following an interminable wait at customs she and Mr. Hitchens were released from the confines of bureaucracy to walk out into a clear, still-cool, fresh morning.

"Sunshine," breathed Mrs. Pollifax happily. Not yet the gold of a tropical noon but a thin radiant silver light that ricocheted down and across the sides of gleaming buildings and scattered rhinestones across the blue harbor. "And there's Hong Kong," she told Mr. Hitchens, pointing across the water to rows of sleek buildings encircling the precipitous slopes of the Peak.

In the bright light Mr. Hitchens's eyes had changed to the intensity of mercury against his dark complexion. "Very charming," he murmured. "Like white cliffs in the sun."

Presently a taxi was whisking them out of Kowloon and down into and through a tunnel, and when they emerged they were on the Hong Kong side. "Which," Mrs. Pollifax reminded Mr. Hitchens, "is all that Britain will have left when mainland China takes back Kowloon and the New Territories in 1997."

"Take back!" he repeated. "You must excuse me but I'm not aware—"

"Well — they've only been leased to Great Britain," she explained. "I believe Hong Kong was settled back in the early 1800s — it all had something to do with the opium trade — and then, being a very small island, only thirty-five square miles in size, and prospering mightily, it leaked over into Kowloon across the harbor, and later a lease was negotiated with mainland China for the New Territories. They tell me the Hong Kong dollar plunges every time Britain and China meet to discuss the change-over in 1997. China is insisting on an agreement this year."

"So it's all quite temporary — one might say like life itself," mused Mr. Hitchens.

She smiled, finding him comfortable to be

with, and feeling that his presence helped her to adjust to Cyrus's absence, too; really, she thought, she had been growing quite spoiled without realizing it.

"But we could almost be in Manhattan," protested Mr. Hitchens. "My white cliffs have turned into banks and office buildings and hotels! Except for the faces on the street—"

She smiled. "Yes, they're different, Hong Kong's population being 98 percent Chinese, but the attaché cases are exactly the same, aren't they?"

"You're certainly very well-informed," he told her.

She did not mention that she had been briefed by Bishop on the long drive to the airport, as well as given a number of colorful anecdotes that might startle him. "Actually I've told you all the facts. But I was here last year, just overnight—"

"I've never been out of the United States before," blurted out Mr. Hitchens.

His confession touched her as well as surprised her; she could remember only too well how disconcerting her own first trip had been, how dazzled and yet oddly insecure she'd felt for the first few days, and she was suddenly very glad that she was breakfasting with him.

Their taxi swept up to the entrance of the

Hong Kong Hilton, they were helped out and their luggage removed at once by porters. They made their way through the first level and then up to the huge lobby where Mr. Hitchens, registering, was given room 601 and Mrs. Pollifax, taking her turn, was given the key to room 614.

"Same floor," murmured Mr. Hitchens.

"Practically neighbors," she agreed. "And — where breakfast?" she inquired of the room clerk.

"The Golden Lotus Room," he told her, leaning forward and pointing.

"I'd dearly love a shave first," said Mr. Hitchens. "Can we meet there in thirty minutes?"

"Fine — and I think, remembering my first visit here, it's buffet, with wonderful papaya and melons."

"I can hardly wait," said Mr. Hitchens.

Mrs. Pollifax found room 614 enormous and filled with light, for which she mentally blessed Bishop. She peered into the small, well-stocked refrigerator in the corner, removed her hat and then sat down on the bed to study the street map of Hong Kong that Bishop had given her, along with rather a lot of Hong Kong money. Feng Imports, he'd told her, was in the city's West Point district, not far from the Man Mo

Temple – Buddhist – tucked away at number 31 Dragon Alley. Its location had been lightly penciled on the map and now Mrs. Pollifax lined it up with the hotel. Obviously a taxi, she realized, as she measured distances, her eye meeting exotic names like Ice House Street, Cotton Tree Drive, Jardine's Bazaar and Yee Wo Street. Definitely not New Jersey, she thought, smiling, and decided that she must reach Dragon Alley before the shop opened so that she could try first to intercept Sheng Ti on the street, before he began work.

Some minutes later Mrs. Pollifax was seated in the same Golden Lotus that she'd enjoyed in June, except that this was very late May of another year. A gracious white-jacketed waiter poured coffee for her and she sipped it while she waited for Mr. Hitchens, admiring the oriental faces around her, the businessmen gesticulating to companions over fact-sheets, the young couples, the obvious tourists with their cameras. When Mr. Hitchens slid into the chair beside her he had changed into slacks and a jacket and looked older, less eccentric and a shade less interesting, but something new had been added: his sober face was animated by excitement.

"You won't believe who I just passed in the lobby," he told her boyishly, "the third-richest man in the world! Western world, that is, and right here in this hotel."

"Now *you're* the well-informed one," she told him. "Who on earth is the third-richest man in the world?"

"His name is—" He frowned. "Oh yes, Lars... Lars Petterson." He grinned. "I turned on my TV as soon as I got into my room and he was being interviewed on Hong Kong television."

"I suppose I have a TV too," she said doubtfully.

He laughed. "I'm addicted to it, very partial to reruns, especially the "I Love Lucy" and "Mary Tyler Moore" shows. Also green bananas," he added, and positively enlivened now he said, "I've been married three times and I think each wife thought a psychic lives an exciting life."

"They didn't expect TV reruns and green bananas?" said Mrs. Pollifax, amused.

"No...oh, thank you," he told the waiter pouring him coffee, and then, his glance wandering, he said eagerly, "There he is now! Just walking into the restaurant."

"Who?" said Mrs. Pollifax.

"Mr. Petterson — you know, the man I was just telling you about."

Mrs. Pollifax wrenched her attention from Mr. Hitchens and her coffee and turned to catch a glimpse of the third-richest man in the world.

"By the door – just entering and talking to the waiter," he told her.

Mrs. Pollifax saw an extremely attractive young man, very tanned and blond, whose slightly bent nose was all that prevented him from being outrageously and wickedly handsome. He wore an orange blazer over silk slacks, a striped blue shirt with an orange cravat tucked into it and Mrs. Pollifax, seeing him, drew in her breath sharply. "*Who* did you say he is?"

"Lars Petterson – Danish, I think, although he talked with an English accent." His glance returned to Mrs. Pollifax and he said, "Is something wrong?"

Mrs. Pollifax, considerably jolted, had begun to smile. "No, nothing – nothing at all," she told him.

But past and present worlds were meeting in collision as she recovered from the shock of recognizing Mr. Lars Petterson, the third-richest man in the Western world, because the man entering the Golden Lotus she knew much better as Robin Burke-Jones, first met in Switzerland where he had been a very successful cat burglar, discreetly relieving sheiks and other wealthy people of their prized gems. For a brief moment a kaleidoscope of vignettes flashed through Mrs. Pollifax's head: of Robin, discovered with her jewelry case, saying "You're not going to blackmail me, then, and you're not going to inform?" Of Robin lowering her on a rope from a balcony to escape a murderer searching for her in the halls; of a long night spent in the Castle Chillon with a small boy and, upon their finding an escape route, Robin's voice emerging from the darkness, "Over here in a rowboat, what took you so long?"

*Dear Robin,* she thought, relishing the jest of seeing him here, for she had also been matron-of-honor at his wedding and only four months ago there had been the usual Christmas card from him and his bride Court.

Except that following his wedding — as she ought to have remembered at once — Robin had abandoned the hazards of cat burglary to become an honest man: he had been invited to use his considerable talents to solve crimes instead of to commit them. He had joined Interpol.

*I wonder,* she thought now, with intense curiosity and considerable amusement, *what he's up to here in Hong Kong...as Lars Petterson, third-richest man in the world.*

# 3

"I believe I'll linger over my coffee a little longer," Mrs. Pollifax told her breakfast companion half an hour later, as he prepared to leave.

"Oh!" said Mr. Hitchens. "Yes, of course." For just a moment he looked a little anxious, and then he nodded and smiled. "Yes. Well. Perhaps since we're both here for only a week we'll find ourselves on the same flight back." He extended his hand. "It's been a real pleasure meeting you."

She stood up to shake his hand. "I wouldn't mind hearing if you successfully locate your missing person," she told him. "Give me a call if you'd like — room 614. If you've time."

His smile was wistful and she remembered that it was his first trip abroad. He would, of course, forget entirely about her once he was swept up by his young Hong Kong friend, but she understood that for just this moment he was experiencing a desire to hang onto the one person familiar to him. "Happy hunting," she told him with a smile, and watched him leave.

Once he was gone she put down her cup of coffee, gathered up her purse and headed for the buffet-island in the center of the room behind which Robin had vanished. She had reached a decision: Robin could not possibly have seen her and she reasoned that it was infinitely kinder that he become aware of her presence now, rather than to be surprised by it later, at some awkward time, since heaven only knew what he might be up to here. Rounding the buffet's southern end her glance sought Robin among the diners and found him: he was seated facing her, talking animatedly to a plump Chinese gentleman at his side. As she appeared beside the pineapples the sudden movement caught his eye and he saw her.

Their eyes met, and for just the fraction of a second he stopped talking, while she in turn allowed her gaze to move through and past him with the indifference of a stranger; then Robin recovered his poise, his glance returned to his companion and he resumed his conversation. But he had seen her — *good*, she thought contentedly, and having established the fact that she was here, and that she would not betray him, she continued past the ham, the eggs, the chafing dishes of omelet, stopped to admire a stunning purple flower and made her exit from the Golden Lotus.

And now for Sheng Ti, she thought, and continued out of the hotel to find a cab.

As she was driven through the streets of Hong Kong she thought back to Sheng Ti, whom she had seen how many times, she wondered: once in the bazaar in Turfan, and twice on that night when she'd begun to realize the KGB was involved, and then one last time in Urumchi, seated beside the road and waiting with the infinite patience of the Chinese, his eyes brightening at the sight of her. She could concede that China had performed miracles for its billion people, but to her Sheng Ti represented the cost of some of those miracles, for he was — she struggled now to remember her impressions — *different*. . .not because his parents had been rich peasants but because of what this had denied him in Mao's China. There had been no chance for him to use his considerable intelligence, there had been first of all the primitive commune to which he'd been sent in central China at the age of sixteen, and from which he'd run away when he was

35

nineteen. For this he'd earned detention and had been sent even deeper into the country, to do roadwork near Urumchi, and here too he'd found it difficult to conform and had acquired a dossier, until at twenty-six, when she'd met him, he had become a nonperson, completely without hope and living by his wits. She had mourned the waste, the rebellions brought about by his incapacity to reduce himself, to repress his intelligence and to abort the talents that shoveling manure and carrying rocks could never satisfy.

In America, she thought, he would have become by now a teacher or a lawyer, for he'd been born curious and Mrs. Pollifax measured intelligence by curiosity, rueing people who never asked questions, never asked why, or what happened next or how. One had not asked questions in Mao's China, and Mao's influence still lingered; one had to conform or be labeled misfit.

And it was she who had urged that Sheng Ti be smuggled out of China with Wang Shen . . . if he was not happy here in Hong Kong, as Bishop had suggested, she wondered if she had done him such a good turn after all.

Some minutes later she was deposited at the foot of a street too narrow for cars, and told by her driver that she would find Dragon Alley halfway up that street, and on the right side. With a feeling of excitement Mrs. Pollifax paid him and stepped out of the cab to be deliciously assaulted, nearly overwhelmed, by noise, people and color. She had found China again, in a corner of Hong Kong far away in time and ambiance from the world of polite commerce in the district that she'd just left.

*Now this,* she thought with pleasure, *is more like it,* and she stood very still, letting the smells and sounds and profusion of colors sweep over her. The narrow street was crammed with narrow buildings from which hung signs of every size and color at wildly juxtaposed angles: TAILOR! SHOES! SILKS! GEMS! COLOUR TV! CURIOS! From balconies above the signs there protruded bamboo poles hung with laundry of every color and description, but mostly of eye-shattering scarlets that matched the other scarlets blazing from suspended banners, lanterns and signs. The street was already filled with people and the sidewalks with street stalls that were heaped with plastic flowers, fresh flowers, sandals, herbs, dried seafood and fresh fruit. The predominant smells were of incense, ginger and fried noodles; the sounds were a cacophony of shrill voices competing with shrill music from blaring radios.

*Lovely,* murmured Mrs. Pollifax, and began

strolling happily up the street through the crowds, stopping at street stalls to peer at jars of pickled snakes, roots of ginseng and souvenir mugs of Hong Kong. Eventually, halfway up the street, and precisely where the cabdriver had promised it, she found Dragon Alley, little more than a broad staircase leading up to another street beyond it. She entered and began to climb.

Number 31 lay on her right, a shabby narrow store with a sign overhead announcing in both Chinese and English the existence of Feng Imports, and the shop window — none too clean, she noted — bore the name of Feng Imports in gold lettering. The door was not open, and drawing abreast of it Mrs. Pollifax shifted her gaze straight ahead and then casually — very casually — glanced at the store window, hesitated and again casually stopped to examine its contents, a display of carved jade and ivory objects.

Very nice, she decided, and certainly more attractive than the exterior of the shop; lifting her eyes she looked beyond the display and into the interior and found it empty. A glance at the door showed her a small hand-lettered sign that told her the shop opened at 10 A.M. It was now 9:40.

Mrs. Pollifax continued up the alley. Number

33 was a shop selling plastic flowers, not yet open; number 35 a narrow house behind a wall; 37 a tailoring establishment with a solitary man hunched over a sewing machine, and 39 the blank wall of a building that fronted on the street at the top of the alley. The opposite side, except for one wholesale store advertising radios, appeared to be narrow wooden houses with balconies and gates, one of them with a sign ROOMS. This latter building, number 40, she noticed, had a bench beside the gate to its rear, and Mrs. Pollifax sat down on it to wait and to watch for Sheng Ti.

At nine forty-five a young girl hurried up Dragon Alley and stopped at Feng Imports, unlocked the door and entered: a very lovely Chinese girl wearing a *cheongsam* of dark blue cotton, her hair very black, her skin very white. Employee number one, decided Mrs. Pollifax.

At ten o'clock a man walked out of Feng Imports, startling Mrs. Pollifax because she had seen no one enter the shop, and strode at a fast pace up the alley toward her. He carried a pigskin overnight bag and was tall and lean, not Chinese, his cheeks pockmarked and his eyes — but she knew what his eyes would look like because she had seen him before: it was the man whom she had inadvertently bumped into on the plane, the man with the black aura.

He passed her quickly without a glance and disappeared into the street above the alley, leaving Mrs. Pollifax to speculate on the co-incidence of his seeking out Feng Imports, too, and obviously before he had stopped any-where else to deposit his luggage. But there was still no sign of Sheng Ti.

At ten fifteen, no one else having entered the shop, Mrs. Pollifax left her bench and strolled down the alley again, trying her best to resemble a wandering tourist. Once again she paused at the window of Feng Imports to look inside. The shop was occupied only by the girl, who was flicking a feathered dust mop over a display of figurines, and Mrs. Pollifax sighed, feeling a large and enveloping yawn in-side of her.

"I'll try again at noon," she told herself and, retracing her steps, she captured a taxi and re-turned to the hotel to unpack and surrender briefly to jet lag.

Promptly at noon, however, she set out again, her hat a shade less squarely on her head and one rose listing slightly in spite of efforts to discipline it; it too suffered from travel fatigue, she guessed. Once again she made her way up Dragon Alley, finding only the shadows changed, and stopped to look into the window and be-yond it: this time she could see two people in the shop, a stooped and elderly Chinese gentleman seated behind the counter, and the girl, now leaning over the counter to rearrange objects on a tray.

There was no Sheng Ti.

At this point Mrs. Pollifax realized that she lacked the patience of a professional spy. She was by nature very direct, and the thought of visiting the shop at hourly intervals for the rest of the week appalled her. Bishop had told her that, on the two occasions when the shop had been reconnoitered, Sheng Ti had been found *inside* it, the first time in the company of Mr. Feng, the second time alone. Where was he now? There was no way to disguise herself and keep the shop under surveillance — she would be noticed at once — and in any case the whole point of her being in Hong Kong was to find and talk with Sheng Ti.

She would go in. Carstairs might not approve but she would go in.

Calmly Mrs. Pollifax entered Feng Imports.

The man seated behind the counter had the face of an ancient Manchu, with skin wrinkled like crepe paper and the ghost of a goatee at his chin; his eyes were nearly suffocated by folds of flesh, but they were shrewd as they moved over the roses on her head and then dropped to her face. She thought he looked tired, like a man

41

who had been seated in this shabby store for all of his life but had once expected a great deal more and had not yet resigned himself to having less.

"Good afternoon," she said cheerfully.

"Good afternoon," he responded, placing his hands in the voluminous sleeves of his robe and bowing slightly.

"I've come to see Sheng Ti," she announced, and waited.

The girl looked up quickly and just as quickly looked away. The man – Mr. Feng, she supposed – stiffened slightly but nothing stirred in his impassive face. "I do not understand," he said politely. "Shangchi?"

"Sheng Ti," repeated Mrs. Pollifax.

To the girl he murmured, his eyes on Mrs. Pollifax, "You may go, Lotus." After another swift and curious glance at Mrs. Pollifax the girl walked to the back of the room, parted the long line of beads that curtained the doorway and disappeared, leaving the beads gently swaying and rustling in her wake. "But," said the man gently, "there is no one here by that name."

*Oh dear,* thought Mrs. Pollifax, *they're going to be difficult, very difficult.* "Nonsense," she said cordially, "of course he's here, I've been told on excellent authority that he works here, and if he no longer works here perhaps you can tell me where he does. Because," she added breathlessly, "I'm on holiday for the week in Hong Kong and really must say hello to him before I leave. You're Mr. Feng?"

"Told he works here?" repeated the man, blinking.

Mrs. Pollifax brought out Bishop's scribbled memo and read from it in a clear loud voice. "Sheng Ti, care of Feng Imports, 31 Dragon Alley...you *are* Mr. Feng?"

He stared curiously at the slip of paper. "If I may see—" His hand reached out with astonishing speed and grasped it before she could either protest or pull back.

He said sharply, *"Who gave you this?"*

"A friend of Sheng Ti's."

"Friend? Of Sheng Ti?"

It felt suddenly important to emphasize that yes, Sheng Ti might have a friend or two. She said tartly, "Is that so surprising, such a charming young man?"

His voice was cool. "And how would such a person as you know such a person as Sheng Ti?"

Even more coolly she said, "I really fail to see how it's any concern of yours, Mr. Feng, but since you insist on an inquisition, I met him in mainland China, near Turfan, in Xinjiang Province. Really," she said sternly, "it was the most appalling situation, and quite a shock to

43

an American tourist, I can assure you. First my meeting Sheng Ti in the marketplace and then the long talk we had—"

He said dryly, "You speak Chinese?"

She waved this aside impatiently. "A companion did, and hearing of his unhappy situation, and then learning he had the opportunity to leave China — but so *illicitly, so dangerously"* — she allowed her voice to falter dramatically — "I have since made every effort — every *effort* — to find out what happened to him." She added in an aggrieved voice, "Which meant knocking on *many* doors and writing a *great* many letters, and *not* taking no for an answer, and I *will* not take no for an answer *now."*

He returned the paper to her. "But you have been misinformed, Mrs. — er—"

"Pollifax."

"Thank you. We are importers here, Mrs. Pollifax, there is no Sheng Ti."

She looked at him squarely, noting that he refused to meet her gaze. "Then why have you asked so many questions? Frankly, sir, I don't believe you."

Behind the beaded curtain she heard a soft laugh; an amused voice said, "Bring our stubborn friend in, Feng."

Mr. Feng's lips thinned. "I don't think—"

"Bring her in." There was a sharpness in the voice that startled Mr. Feng, who shrugged, turned toward the curtain and gestured Mrs. Pollifax to follow him.

The multicolored beads slithered and whispered again. Mrs. Pollifax entered a cubbyhole of an office where the girl Lotus was seated now at a desk stringing what looked to be pearls. The man who had eavesdropped from behind the curtain led her through this room, presenting only his back to her, but she could see that he was a large man wearing a well-tailored silk suit and that he limped slightly.

The room they entered made her blink, its brightness startling after the dimness of the shop. A huge window had been set very high into one wall, at a slant to catch the north light; two walls were lined with shelves of exquisite ancient jade and ivory figurines, another with wooden packing cartons, and under the window ran a bench and long table on which she saw a pile of glittering small stones.

But the stranger interested her more and she turned quickly to look at him.

He bowed slightly. "Pray sit down," he said, and to the man behind her, "That will be all, Mr. Feng." He moved behind a small desk in the corner and gestured her to one of the chairs nearby.

Mrs. Pollifax guessed that he was Eurasian, and therefore Mr. Detwiler, although only the shape of his eyes suggested an oriental parent. His face was broad and fleshy, the nose flat and his mouth very wide, the thin lips turning upward at each corner and giving him a very pleasant look but also a Buddha-like smile that appeared fixed and immutable. His suit was black, his shirt a gleaming white and she noticed gold cuff links at the wrists and a modest gold pin at his tie. A faint aroma of musk reached her from where he sat.

She told him firmly, "I'm looking for Sheng Ti — as you may have heard."

"Yes indeed," he said, his smile deepening slightly. "But what do you want of this Sheng Ti?"

"To make sure that he's well and happy," she said promptly, "but — if I may be frank?"

"But of course," he said with an encouraging nod.

Without the slightest twinge of conscience Mrs. Pollifax produced the *piéce de résistance* that she had worked over during her passage from the shop into this room. "Well," she said, leaning forward confidentially, "I went to a great deal of trouble to find him because he weighed terribly on my mind. I went back to the States, where I am currently president of

46

my garden club, and I told them about Sheng Ti and," she told him in triumph, "they have voted to sponsor his entry into the United States!"

"You have indeed been busy," he said, his eyes watching her face with interest. "May I see the paper with its directions to Sheng Ti?"

"Of course," she said, handing over Bishop's memo again. "*Is* Sheng Ti here?"

The man studied the memo. "How *exactly* did you get this?" he asked.

Mrs. Pollifax drew a deep breath and sailed in. "Well, I knew the name of the American with whom Sheng Ti was leaving China, you see, and so I tracked him down, and he told me that Sheng Ti had been left in Hong Kong, and he gave me an address – in Washington, of all places!" she added innocently. "And finally – after many very insistent letters and calls – it was all very strange – I was given this."

The man stared at the memo and nodded. "You could have received this from only one source, no one else could possibly know of Sheng Ti's presence here."

"He *is* here, then!"

"Oh yes," he said smoothly, handing her back the memo with a smile, "but it has of course been infinitely mysterious to us, your

47

knowing of his presence. You are visiting Hong Kong for how long?" he asked politely.

"A week. To see the flowers. I myself have won a number of prizes for my geraniums and—"

"Yes," he said, interrupting her and leaning forward, "but you must drop the idea of seeing Sheng Ti, if you please. He is quite well — working hard — and I really have to insist that he not be distracted by seeing you."

"Not see him!" cried Mrs. Pollifax in her best shocked voice. "But I've come so far, and I thought — my garden club thought—"

"But he is very happy here," Detwiler assured her smoothly. "Perhaps later, another year, but he is useful to me and once he has learned more English he will be even more useful. I intend," he said softly but firmly, "to keep him here. For the moment, anyway," he added in a more conciliatory voice.

Mrs. Pollifax said darkly, "He hoped to go to school, are you sending him to school? And to learn a trade, too, and—"

He said gently, "On that score you may rest. He is being taught English, yes, and also something of jade and diamonds. Come and see," he said, rising and pointing to the workbench. "There are perhaps a hundred thousand U.S. dollars' worth of diamonds here, something you may never see again."

Mrs. Pollifax started to protest, knowing very well that she was being diverted, but, feeling that she had at least entered the dragons' den and met the head dragon, she allowed herself the diversion. "May I inquire your name?" she asked sweetly. "I believe you already know mine is Mrs. Pollifax."

He said absently, "Detwiler, but just look at this stone, will you? Five carats — beautifully cut and polished."

"You sell them here in your shop?" she asked.

"Oh no, they're sent all over the world. These particular stones were cut in Antwerp and sent here to Hong Kong to be polished...Hong Kong imports millions of dollars' worth of diamonds to be finished. These...who knows? Lotus has the invoices and could tell us but they will go to many places: Egypt, Saudi Arabia, Japan..." He shrugged. "But allow me to give you a small souvenir of your visit to Hong Kong. Not a diamond, of course, but something still rather special. To not leave disappointed."

"Oh?"

"Or empty-handed — I insist." He moved to the shelves of ivory and jade objects, picked out a jade figurine, shook his head, returned it to the shelf and selected another, holding it out to

Mrs. Pollifax. "Ivory," he said softly. "Is it not beautiful?"

"A Buddha!" she gasped. "How lovely!" The figure was roughly twelve inches tall and a masterpiece of intricate carving, the Buddha seated in the traditional lotus position, the hands carved in exquisite detail. On his head he wore an unusual headdress that rose to a peak – a triumph of craftsmanship in its delicate lacelike detail – while the folds of his robe fell in very simple lines and the face was utterly serene.

"Please – it is yours," he told her. "It is as valuable as Sheng Ti is to me, and as valuable as your concern for him. In appreciation of your concern."

"How very disarming of you," said Mrs. Pollifax, feeling not at all disarmed and already wondering what she would do next to find Sheng Ti. "And how lovely of you to do this," she added.

"Lotus," he called, "come and take this to Mr. Feng to wrap for the lady."

The girl came at once, giving Mrs. Pollifax another curious glance, and left the room carrying the Buddha.

"Well," said Mrs. Pollifax with a sigh, "I mustn't take up any more of your time – or mine, either – for there's so much to *see* in Hong Kong." She shook her head. "But my garden club is going to be heartbroken, although if he really is learning a trade, and is happy — you're sure?"

"That," said Detwiler smoothly, "I can assure you of most sincerely, Mrs. Pollifax."

"But I do wonder," she said, feeling that her act needed one last touch, "if you would have any objections if members of the garden club wrote to Sheng Ti from the United States? He could become" — she swallowed her dismay at the expression and hurled it at him — "a *pen pal?*"

"No objections at all," said Detwiler, looking relieved. "A most auspicious way for him to practice his English, and Sheng Ti would be touched, I know."

Mrs. Pollifax composed her face into an agreeable mask, shook his hand, murmured her pleasure at meeting him, her apologies for interrupting him, her gratitude at the gift and moved toward the office and then through the beaded curtains. Here a man stood waiting, a young Chinese wearing a flawlessly cut dark business suit and carrying an attaché case. At sight of Detwiler he brightened, bowed, and bushed past Mrs. Pollifax to enter the inner sanctum that she'd just left.

Mr. Feng held out her package wrapped in white paper. "Your gift," he said, his face still impassive, a mask concealing what, she wondered, resentment, suspicion, anger?

"Thank you," she said and walked out, glad to relax her own mask that she knew very well concealed resentment, frustration and anger.

But if Mrs. Pollifax left Feng Imports feeling definitely ruffled she in no way conceded defeat; her initial foray might have failed, but this only meant that she must find another way to contact Sheng Ti. The fact that she had no idea of what her next ploy might be only proved to her that a brief period of gestation was needed: she would forget Sheng Ti for the moment and do some sightseeing.

She could not, however, forget either Mr. Feng or Mr. Detwiler, and as she walked in the direction of Queen's Road Central she sorted out some rather confused impressions. It struck her as extremely odd that Mr. Detwiler had intervened following Mr. Feng's flat denial of knowing Sheng Ti. She found it interesting to speculate on why Detwiler had bothered at all to intercede, to invite her behind the beaded curtains and proceed to make a liar out of Mr. Feng. She wondered what he'd hoped to gain by this, since for herself the results were the same: she was not to be allowed to see Sheng Ti. It certainly implied a few conflicts at Feng Imports, but since any conflicts they might have

52

were not her assignment she decided that this too had better be put aside.

Or so she had decided until she realized that she was being followed...

At first the streets had been too crowded for this suspicion to dawn on her, but as she turned corners and the crowds thinned, and as she began to stop occasionally to glance into shop windows at rugs and vases, she became increasingly aware that among the people strolling behind her one of them stopped each time that she stopped. It was a matter of peripheral vision and of suspended motion, rather like a child's game of Statues, where two people froze at a given signal but only one was supposed to do it. When she stopped for the fourth time, deliberately, it was to steal a glance behind her, and she was surprised to recognize her surveillant: it was the young man with the attaché case who had been waiting for Detwiler when she emerged from the beaded curtains.

The realization that Detwiler had put a tail on her pleased and even exhilarated her. *Good,* she thought, *I've worried them, they want to be sure that I'm exactly who I say I am, a simple American garden-club tourist made happy by the promise that Sheng Ti can have pen pals.* Her lip curled — as if they'd allow him that — and hard on the heels of this thought she realized what she'd not yet fully acknowledged: Sheng Ti was as much a captive at Feng Imports as if he'd been placed in a prison. He *was* in a prison.

Finding herself at last on Queen's Road Central Mrs. Pollifax silently vowed that she would return to haunt Feng Imports even if she had to disguise herself as she had done in Turfan: as a Chinese peasant woman, a bandanna around her head, eyes pulled into a slant, sandals flapping on her feet...she smiled at the memory. First of all, however, she must play out her role as Innocent Tourist, and after consulting her map she began walking up Queen's Road determined to bore and to exhaust the man behind her as quickly and totally as possible.

Hours later Mrs. Pollifax had succeeded only in exhausting herself. She had done a great deal of walking, all of it without lunch; she had bought Cyrus a silk tie that she might just as well have bought for him at home; she had taken a cab to the Zoological and Botanic Gardens and had thoroughly explored them, paying special attention to the aviary that Cyrus would want to hear about in detail, and making notes for him in her memo pad about drongos, grebes, herons, babblers and kites. Eventually she had found her way to the Peak Tramway where she had been happy to sit in the cable car and watch the city drop slowly away, level by level, as it bore her to the top of Victoria Peak.

Now, at nearly six o'clock in the afternoon, she sat on a bench 1,809 feet above Hong Kong and looked down at the city, its buildings crowded into what looked to be an incredibly narrow strip of land between the Peak and the water. She admired the great expanse of intensely blue harbor with its ferries scooting about like water bugs, and presently she leaned over to remove her shoes and blissfully wriggle her toes. When a playful wind tugged at her hat she removed it, too. Glancing off to her right she saw that the Man with the Attaché Case had also found a bench and she was about to concede victory to him — although not without resentment — when she saw him lean over and remove his shoes, too. Human after all, she thought, and at once both her tired feet and her hunger seemed small sacrifices to have made; she sat and contentedly rested, allowing herself to think ahead to a very good dinner, a long soak in a hot tub, followed by a few Yoga exercises and then some very concentrated thinking on what to do next about Sheng Ti.

Idly she looked down at the packages she had carried all over Hong Kong: Cyrus's tie and the ivory Buddha, and on impulse she unwrapped the tie and held it up to the light. Did

Cyrus like this particular shade of blue, she wondered now, doubtfully, and then she put it aside to unwrap the Buddha, eager to see its superb carving again.

Drawing it from its string and wrappings she noticed a thin slip of rice paper taped across the Buddha's right hand and with a frown she tore it loose. She was about to toss it into the wind when she noticed words written in tiny script on the rice paper. Curious, she held it closer and read:

*If you want to see Sheng Ti he sleeps at 40 Dragon Alley in shed at back, after 10 P.M.*

# 4

In a state of considerable astonishment Mrs. Pollifax slipped her feet back into her shoes and without exploring the Peak any further, without even venturing into the tower, she boarded the next tram back into the city.

"How...?" she asked herself, and then, "*who*...?" and then, "when...?"

As the cable car descended at what seemed a perpendicular slant, she gazed unseeingly at the tops of green trees and the roofs of villas hugging the sides of the mountain and reconstructed the scene in her mind. Mr. Detwiler had removed the Buddha from her grasp and summoned the girl Lotus; it was not likely the message had come from him after his refusing to produce Sheng Ti. "Have Mr. Feng wrap this," he'd told the girl, but she could not conceive of Mr. Feng adding the message to the Buddha, either, when he'd not even cared to admit Sheng Ti's existence.

The tram reached the bottom and Mrs. Pollifax made her exit, crossed the boulevard and limped wearily down Garden Road toward the Hong Kong Hilton. Her reasoning had eliminated all but the girl Lotus, in which case — if it was she who had attached the rice paper to the figurine — she must have been eavesdropping and have heard everything said in the back room.

They all eavesdrop there, she thought crossly. First Mr. Detwiler, then the girl...had Mr. Feng also listened in somehow to her conversation with Detwiler?

The Man with the Attaché Case was still behind her as she reached the Garden Road entrance to the hotel, and she resisted the urge to wave to him and tell him that he could have his dinner now. It seemed a pity to curb such an insouciant gesture, she thought; after all, they had spent the afternoon together sharing a number of interesting experiences, his feet hurt and he must be as hungry as she was, but she reminded herself that he would feel a dreadful failure if he discovered that he'd been noticed. She wondered if he would be waiting for her when she ventured out again at ten o'clock to find Sheng Ti.

He was still behind her when she walked

through the entrance and found herself at ground level in a mall of shops filled with all kinds of glamorous objects: cameras, watches, gems, rugs, curios. Hurrying along, eager now to get to her room, she passed a shop featuring objets d'art with a Buddha in its window very similar to her own, and with its price tag conspicuously displayed. Mrs. Pollifax stopped, and rather sheepishly walked over to the window to examine both the Buddha and its price tag. She found the Buddha definitely inferior to her own and yet it bore the price of — here she did hasty calculations in her head and was shocked to discover that in U.S. money the ivory Buddha in the window cost almost seven hundred dollars.

She thought crossly, *I think I need that very hot bath now because I am receiving too many jolts...Mr. Detwiler — who is suspected by Carstairs of being a traitor — has just presented me with a carved Buddha worth a great deal of money...No one at Feng Imports will tell me a thing about Sheng Ti and yet his address turns up in a package like the message in a fortune cookie...I'm being followed and don't know why...The gift can be a bribe, the address on the rice paper a trap...*

With her surveillant trailing despondently behind her Mrs. Pollifax rode up the escalator to the main lobby where she picked up her key at the desk and entered the elevator. Her last glimpse of The Man with the Attaché Case was of him sinking gratefully into a soft and embracing chair, while in turn she was grateful that he couldn't follow her into her room to see her, too, sink gratefully into a soft chair.

By nine o'clock, however, Mrs. Pollifax had thoroughly revived. Having treated herself to dinner in her own room, as befitted a person afflicted by jet lag and by conflicting signals from Feng Imports, she was ready for her nocturnal adventure. No garden-of-roses hat tonight: she tied a dark kerchief around her head to match her dark slacks and open-neck shirt, and after tucking map and flashlight into her purse she proceeded to plot a zigzag exit from the hotel, taking the elevator to the second floor and then the staircase down to the lobby. Here she made an open dash to the escalator that deposited her in the mall at the lower level, where she browsed through the shops that were still open, spent a few minutes watching two giggling young women take their blood pressure at a machine placed in the mall for that purpose, was enchanted by all the flashing lights and marveled at such an invention. Certain at last that she wasn't being followed she walked out into the street, continued walking for several blocks before hailing a taxi and was driven through streets ablaze with gaudy reds, golds and glittering white neon: Hong Kong at night.

It was ten minutes past the hour when she stumbled over the bench on which she'd sat this morning; Dragon Alley was distressingly dark, its windows shuttered and barred for the night. She discreetly shone her flashlight just once, at number 40's gate, and then opened it to enter the backyard. It was brighter inside here than in the street, for lights as well as music spilled over from what appeared to be the rear of a nightclub in the next building. In the reflected radiance she could see the silhouette of a small hut or shed and a slim figure seated on a bench outside of it. Mrs. Pollifax moved toward the figure cautiously.

"*Oh!*" gasped the figure and jumped up. It was the girl Lotus, her white skin gleaming like porcelain in the dim light.

"So it *was* you," whispered Mrs. Pollifax.

Lotus whispered back, "Follow me — it's not safe here! Ssh — very quiet please."

Mrs. Pollifax obediently followed her into the deeper shadows and past the shed to the rear of the nightclub or restaurant that adjoined the yard. A door was opened, she was led into a dark hall and then into a room on the left that was illuminated by a solitary oil lamp on a table. Sitting nervously beside the table, looking ready to bolt at any moment, was Sheng Ti.

"*Xiānsbeng!*" he cried, springing to his feet. "I could not believe!"

Mrs. Pollifax, laughing, grasped his outstretched hands. "It's me — I mean it's I, Sheng Ti. Isn't this a surprise, isn't it wonderful?" But even as she greeted him she was shocked by his appearance: he was a young man whose attractive round face was made to be cheerful and lively, but his face was haggard now, the eyes dulled by worry. "Sheng Ti," she said, "they wouldn't let me see you, why?"

He burst into a torrent of Chinese until Mrs. Pollifax turned questioningly to Lotus.

The girl placed a steadying hand on Sheng Ti's arm. "Please — sit down," she said, indicating three chairs neatly arranged at the table.

It was a little like meeting in a cave, thought Mrs. Pollifax, glancing around the small room. A blanket had been hung over the one small window in the wall and the oil lamp cast flickering shadows over them and turned their faces a dull gold. "Why?" she repeated. "Why didn't they want me to see you?"

Sheng Ti sucked in his breath with a small

hissing sound. "If they know I see you now—"

"Yes?"

"They would *kill.*"

Startled Mrs. Pollifax turned to Lotus. "You believe this?"

"Oh yes," the girl said simply. "Something is very wrong now at 31 Dragon Alley, you know? It was a small thing at first, just a whisper for me, until I began to speak with Sheng Ti and then we became friends—"

"We love," put in Sheng Ti.

Lotus blushed and smiled. "Yes, we love each other — this happened and it is very beautiful, this — but we have to meet secretly, you know? And when I learn what they ask of him" — she shook her head — "something is very wrong."

"What do they ask of him?" demanded Mrs. Pollifax. "Tell me. Please. It's important."

Sheng Ti began haltingly. "At first very okay," he said. "I come here before Lantern Festival—"

"September," put in Lotus.

"Yes. And worked in shop, oh *very* okay. But near new year—" He shook his head. "Everything change. Many fights have Mr. Feng and Mr. Detwiler, I hear them behind door. And then they give me new jobs." Obviously frustrated by his new English he turned and spoke to Lotus in Chinese.

"He says," continued Lotus for him, "that he

63

did not mind stealing back in Turfan, in mainland China, because it was to keep alive, but as you know he hoped by leaving China he could go to school and learn."

Mrs. Pollifax nodded. "Yes, and what is his new job?"

"Stealing," Lotus said. "For two months he was taught by a man named Hoong to pick pockets and now they have put him to work stealing from people's pockets."

"They *what?*" gasped Mrs. Pollifax.

Sheng Ti nodded. "Everything hell now, bloody hell. Mr. Detwiler hit me. Very nasty all the time. Mr. Feng has to run things more and nasty, too. Mr. Detwiler take heroin now," he said. "I see once — the long needle and white powder. He hit me *again* when I see."

"Oh dear!" murmured Mrs. Pollifax with feeling.

"Yes."

"But what do they have you stealing?" she asked.

"Passports," he told her.

This was unexpected. "Passports?" she repeated. "Not money?" He shook his head, and fumbling for the rationale behind this she said, "How many? What kinds? From whom?"

Lotus answered for him. "He does not tell me all he does but I know this: they give him a

64

very elegant suit and shoes and tie and they send him to the Government House or sometimes to the airport and twice I have seen the passports he stole. One was Bulgarian, one Canadian." Sheng Ti spoke and she nodded. "He says he's stolen eleven of them now for Mr. Detwiler."

"Eleven," murmured Mrs. Pollifax, frowning over this.

"I would not know anything if Sheng Ti and I had not spoken," confided Lotus. "Everything is hidden, concealed from me, for I do invoices, letters, and dust the shop. But I have heard the quarrels between Mr. Feng and Mr. Detwiler, heard the sound of them at least, and—" She shook her head. "There is something very wrong. Sheng Ti would like to run away but they've taken all his papers and how can he go anywhere without papers?"

Mrs. Pollifax leaned forward and said earnestly, "Don't let him run away, ask him please to stay and help. Because the people who sent him to Feng Imports *know* something is wrong — it's why I'm here."

"And they will help you," she said, turning to Sheng Ti, "if you help *them.*" She was remembering Bishop saying, *We're prepared to offer him immigration to the United States but only if he gives fair value in return, it has to be*

65

*earned, there has to be enough.* She dared not speak of it, for there was not enough, not yet. "Could you learn more?" she asked of Sheng Ti. "Could you follow Mr. Detwiler, find out where he goes, whom he sees? If you can get information for me I promise you that you'll have your papers back, and a new job, and schooling...I've been told I may promise you this. But first — first it has become terribly important to find out what's happening at Feng Imports, and only you can do this."

Sheng Ti frowned; he looked at Lotus, his eyes questioning, and then he gave a bitter laugh. "Why do I stop to think? I would do anything to get away, anything. And you give me hope?" He spoke to Lotus in Chinese and she nodded.

"He will do this. And I too if I can."

"Good. They don't suspect me — I don't think — except why did they have me followed this morning after I left the shop?"

Immediately she was sorry she had mentioned this because Sheng Ti leaped to his feet looking terrified. "You were followed? Followed *here?*" he cried.

"No, this morning, after leaving the shop. I promise you no one followed me here tonight," she told him.

"But they may still — I must go," he said

desperately. "Oh my God. Please — what is to be done?"

"Do sit down," begged Mrs. Pollifax.

"No — let him go," Lotus said. "Go back to number 40, Sheng, you haven't slept for two nights, I will tell you later what she says."

He managed a wan smile, but he left, nevertheless, after one anguished look of entreaty at Mrs. Pollifax.

"They have not frightened you?" she asked Lotus.

"No, but I am frightened for Sheng Ti," the girl said. "He is afraid of being sent back to mainland China, where he'd certainly be placed in a labor camp this time. It is very serious to have no papers, you know?"

Someone knocked on the door and Mrs. Pollifax discovered the atmosphere had so infected her that she, too, jumped and turned a startled face to Lotus. The girl went to the door and opened it an inch, speaking in Chinese to whoever was in the hall. When she returned, closing the door behind her, she said, "I sleep here with two other girls, I had to pay them to stay away but now they want to go to their beds." She said anxiously, "You will have to go, but what am I to tell Sheng Ti?"

Mrs. Pollifax brought out her memo pad and wrote in it, tore out the sheet and handed it to her. "This is my name," she told her, "and this is where I'm staying, and that's my room number. Both you and Sheng Ti had better memorize this and burn it." She shook her head. "We simply *must* find some other way to meet. Could one of you phone me tomorrow night at ten o'clock at my hotel?"

Lotus nodded. "Tomorrow night, ten o'clock." Some of the anxiety in her face had cleared, leaving it grave and lovely again; she said shyly, "I'm glad you're here, I'm glad someone knows, it's been so lonely." With one hand on the door she turned and added, "He will work hard for you now, too — you will see." With the slip of paper tucked into her sleeve she opened the door and peered out. "Come," she whispered, "you can leave through this building, through the kitchen. I show you."

Once out on the street Mrs. Pollifax's first reaction was to draw a deep sigh of relief and to admit how glad she was to leave the small dim room that had been filled — *glutted,* she thought — with Sheng Ti's fear and Lotus's anxiety. It was not a happy thought to realize that he must risk even more danger before he could be lifted out of Feng Imports; she would much prefer to have carried him away with her to place on the next flight to San Francisco but this thought only reminded her ruefully of how spoiled Americans could be: Sheng Ti lived the precarious life of a refugee, still without papers or identity.

Her garden club, she decided grimly, was very definitely going to have to sponsor Sheng Ti — she would insist on it — and Lotus too, if their relationship continued. In the meantime she had to make sure that Sheng Ti survived physically...It was possible that heroin was the explanation for Mr. Detwiler's sloppy reports to Carstairs's department over the past two months but she did not like the sound of those eleven stolen passports. She shook her head over it; no, she did not like the sound of that at *all*.

Flagging down a taxi Mrs. Pollifax rode back to the hotel and entered this time by the front entrance, boldly, and once again rose in the elevator to room 614. Here she tossed her purse on the bed and went to the telephone where she dictated a cable to Carstairs at the cover address in Baltimore: FRIENDSHIP RENEWED, WEATHER CLOUDY, EMILY POLLIFAX. When she replaced the receiver she saw by her travel clock that it was half-past eleven, and reflecting on what a long day it had been, she crossed the room to her suitcase.

Drawing out pajamas and cold cream she

suddenly stiffened as something hit her door with a violent thud.

With a frown she dropped the pajamas and moved to the door. "Who is it?" she called.

There was no answer.

Cautiously Mrs. Pollifax released the lock and the door flew open, almost knocking her down as a man fell into her arms with blood streaming down his face. As she instinctively recoiled he slid to the floor and sprawled at her feet.

She stared down at him, appalled: it was Mr. Hitchens.

# 5

Mrs. Pollifax's initial reaction was astonishment: one talked with people on planes; one might even share a casual breakfast with them, but following this one did not expect to see them again, and certainly not late at night bleeding on the floor at one's feet. Accepting reality, however — for definitely Mr. Hitchens was *here* — she pushed the door closed and knelt beside him, one hand reaching out to gingerly explore what lay beneath his blood-matted hair.

Wincing at what she found she sped into the bathroom for towels, returned with a wet one and a dry one, pressed the dry towel to the bloody gash in his scalp and applied the wet one to the lines of scarlet lacing his right cheek like deranged embroidery.

His eyes were closed but his lips had begun to move. "Something..."

She leaned closer to hear him.

"...terribly wrong," he whispered. "How...
*how*..."

"Don't try to talk," she told him, "I'll call a
doctor."

"No," he gasped, rousing at this and suddenly
opening those strange silver eyes. "Not safe.
After me. How — must find how..."

His eyes closed and he lapsed again into unconsciousness while Mrs. Pollifax stared at him
and considered his words, weighing the gash in
his head against his panic. She did not believe
that he would die from the blow but on the
other hand he might very well die from infec-
tion if unattended. His panic, however, she
implicitly believed in; his very presence here
proved that he was terrified, for this was, after
all, the Hong Kong Hilton where every amenity
was available, yet he'd chosen to come to her
room. For that matter he could scarcely have
come far, she realized, for no one could possibly have wandered through the hotel's lobby
in such a state without causing pandemonium.

It must have happened in his room, she
thought, and — *not safe*, he'd said. Did he
mean that he might have been followed?

She had closed the door but not locked it;
now she jumped up to snap the lock but as it
slammed into place with a *ping!* she became

aware of movement outside in the hall. Her eyes fell to the door knob and to her horror she saw it turn slowly, silently, to the left and then to the right, accompanied by a subtle sound of metal probing metal.

Mrs. Pollifax forced down a scream. *Except I want to scream,* she cried silently, watching the knob twist back and forth, *"I wantoscream I wantoscream I wantoscream . . ."*

The door opened and Robin Burke-Jones stepped into the room, closing the door behind him. "I do hope I'm not interrupting anything," he said cheerfully, "I saw you cross the lobby a few minutes ago and—" His glance fell to the man lying at her feet. "Good God!" he exclaimed. "Been at your karate again? Who on earth—!"

Thoroughly shaken Mrs. Pollifax stammered, "N-not karate, it's Mr. H-H-Hitchens, he just sort of f-fell into my room terrified of being f-f-followed, and then you — then you—"

Robin whistled. "And you thought — I say, I'm frightfully sorry. The thing is, I'm being followed, too, and I simply couldn't afford to knock on your door and stand around waiting for it to open." Regarding Mr. Hitchens with considerable fascination he said, "Chap needs a doctor, doesn't he?"

She'd forgotten the crisp British accent Robin

had worked so hard to acquire. "He begged me not to call one."

"You know him, of course."

"Scarcely this well," she told him. "That is, we flew in on the same plane, where we had a very interesting talk about psychic phenomena — he's a psychic, you see, he's come here to find a missing person — and then we had breakfast together this morning, I think it was this morning although it seems forever ago, but I certainly didn't expect to see him again."

"And now he's here."

"Yes, now he's here."

Robin knelt beside Mr. Hitchens. "Nasty bash, this...someone did a damn good job on him, but if he could still utter words and all that, it's promising. If he was capable of talking how exactly did he explain his — er — impetuous arrival?"

Mrs. Pollifax closed her eyes and thought about it. "First he whispered 'something terribly wrong...how...how' and then when I told him I'd call a doctor he gasped 'Not safe... after me...how...must find how....' "

Robin stood up and gave her a thoroughly startled look. "Would you mind repeating that, word for word?"

Obligingly she repeated it. "Why?"

Robin's eyes had narrowed. "And you say

he's here to find a missing person?"

She nodded. "What is it, Robin?"

Ignoring this he said thoughtfully, "I can provide a doctor who won't ask questions and I think I'd like very much to stick around and hear what else your friend Mr. Hitchens has to say when he regains consciousness." He walked over to the phone, dialed a number and stood waiting, smiling at her. "And to think," he told her, shaking his head, "that I stopped in just to say hello and talk over old times! You know, such as how you rescued young Hafez and karate-chopped the sheik's men and — hello, Chiang?" he said into the phone. "Three-oh-one here, I'm at the hotel; can you come discreetly to room 614 — repeat, 614? Chap with possible concussion, unconscious at the moment, bad gash in the head, probably needs stitching...Right-oh. Good." He hung up. "He'll be here in five minutes. You know, it crossed my mind when I saw your friend here that it might be Cyrus, but you wrote us that Cyrus is six feet four, and this chap simply doesn't extend that far on the floor."

"He's bird-watching," she told him. "In Vermont. Is this conversation making any sense? I had to leave in a great hurry and—"

"So you *are* on a job for Carstairs!"

75

She smiled. "A very small one," she admitted. "Reconnaissance, you might say. Robin, what startled you when I quoted Mr. Hitchens's words to you, and why do you want to hear what he has to say when he wakes up?"

Robin perched on the arm of a chair and looked at her. "I am naturally sworn to secrecy but considering that I owe you my lovely bride and my new job — what startled me, my dear Mrs. P., is that for the past two days I've been looking for a missing man who happens to be named Hao."

It was her turn to be startled. "Named... You mean — you mean 'must find how' could be a name?"

He smiled. "In Hong Kong, yes. Hong Kong is filled with Hu's and Hao's and Yu's and Wi's...It could of course be coincidence—"

"And your name for this occasion is Lars Petterson?"

"Oh you know that, do you." He looked amused.

"Actually it was Mr. Hitchens who told me at breakfast, he'd just seen you on Hong Kong television this morning before you walked into the restaurant." She shook her head at him. "Third-richest man in the *world*, Robin?"

"Mmmm," he murmured, grinning. "It was hoped that it might bring just the right kind of attention — or wrong kind, whichever way you look at it — my arriving with great fanfare and lots of money to invest, possibly very naïve and definitely a playboy."

"And now you're being followed?"

"Only since I began looking for the missing Mr. Hao, which is interesting, don't you think?"

She stared at him thoughtfully and then she said, "All right, why are you here, Robin?"

His face sobered. "To put it very simply I'm here because there's something terribly wrong in Hong Kong...disturbingly and alarmingly wrong, and I'm here to discover what it is."

There was silence and then Mrs. Pollifax said musingly, "You know, that's the third time today that someone's told me something is 'terribly wrong': you, Mr. Hitchens, and someone I talked with earlier this evening. In your case, Robin—"

"That will be Chiang," Robin said as three staccato knocks interrupted her. "Let me open it, he knows me."

Dr. Chiang hurried into the room, a diminutive man in a nearly threadbare suit. He gave Mrs. Pollifax one quick, curious glance before he opened up his medical kit, and then he knelt beside Mr. Hitchens, who stirred, groaned, opened his eyes and began to gag.

"Basin," called Dr. Chiang imperatively, and

Mrs. Pollifax, lacking a basin, flew to the waste-basket and extracted a plastic bag.

Presently, after Mr. Hitchens had been thoroughly sick, he was carried to the chaise longue where Dr. Chiang began to deal expertly with his wound: cleaning, sterilizing, applying a local anesthetic and then eight stitches. "He'll be all right," Dr. Chiang said at last, stepping back to observe his patient. "No concussion... He's lucky because he was hit hard but fortunately not in a really vulnerable area, although he's going to have one hell of a headache. I've given him a tetanus shot, an antibiotic and something to relax him. If he's still restless in an hour try him on a little brandy but nothing else until morning."

"Thanks, Chiang," said Robin.

The doctor gave Mrs. Pollifax a second interested and curious glance. "Husband?"

She shook her head. "Oh no."

Dr. Chiang looked amused. "I see, yes... well — good luck and call me if you need me."

"Nice," said Mrs. Pollifax when he'd gone. "It's just that he doesn't *look* like a doctor somehow."

Robin laughed. "In about four years' time he just may find a free hour to shop for a new suit, or then again he may not. A good man, Chiang — does a great deal of work with the boat people over in Aberdeen. Harvard Medical School, actually. By the way he *did* mention brandy, didn't he? Because frankly I could use some fortifying myself, it's beginning to feel like a *very* long day."

Mrs. Pollifax hurried to the small refrigerator and inspected its contents. "Did you find your refrigerator crammed full of food and drink when you arrived, too?"

"Ah yes," said Robin, "but I must warn you, they keep a very efficient eye on what's removed."

"How deflating," she said. "But I see a sample bottle of champagne, of white wine, and – ah yes, brandy." She brought it to Robin with a glass, after which they sat and looked expectantly at Mr. Hitchens, who was staring at them with considerable bewilderment.

"I'm Mrs. Pollifax," she reminded him, leaning forward and speaking in a clear firm voice. "We met on the plane and flew into Hong Kong together and shared breakfast, remember? And this is – uh – Mr. Petterson, who happened to be – er – passing by, and who happens to be looking for a man named Mr. Hao."

Mr. Hitchens turned his silver eyes on Robin and examined him; if he recognized him as Third Richest Man in the World he gave no sign. He said, "Damien Hao?"

Mrs. Pollifax heard Robin's quick intake of breath but his voice when he spoke was calm. "Damien Hao, yes. I believe you've been looking for him too?"

Mr. Hitchens made the mistake of nodding, promptly groaned and clutched his head. "Got hit – in my room," he explained and then his voice turned urgent. "Alec, where's Alec?"

Robin said quietly, "That would be Inspector Hao's son, Alec?"

"Yes – *yes!* Asked me to find his father. With me all day."

Mrs. Pollifax, weaving certain threads together, said eagerly, "He told me one of his former students at Boston University begged him to come here to find a missing relative. Robin, who is Damien Hao?"

"He *was* the head of Hong Kong's specially formed police unit to investigate drugs, crime and corruption," said Robin grimly. "I say 'was' because he suddenly resigned three weeks ago in the midst of rumors that he'd been found in some sort of compromising situation. He resigned, he said, to clear his name and – as he phrased it – to continue his own private investigations. It was headline news because he's known for his rocklike integrity, and the Governor, whom I interviewed, feels personally that Hao was framed. And then ten days ago he disappeared."

Mrs. Pollifax turned to Mr. Hitchens. "Did you find him today?"

The silver eyes closed. "No...used a map—"

"Yes?"

Mr. Hitchens sighed. "Saw...visioned... place he'd been...hut or barn, green fields, water wheel in distance...we drove, Alec and I...place called New Territories."

"Go on," Robin urged, nodding.

"...growing dark...saw it."

"Saw the hut and the water wheel," prompted Mrs. Pollifax.

Mr. Hitchens opened his eyes. "Yes. And walked...searched it. Very small, earth floor, and then, and then..." A look of pain crossed his face. "A man — a farmer we thought — came to see who we were and...when I woke up Alec was gone." His voice ended in a weak sob. "So I walked and walked...too woozy for Alec's car...walked...a taxi...can't remember and then...my room...hotel room. And someone there. In dark. Pow."

Puzzled, Mrs. Pollifax said, "This farmer — you went to *sleep?*"

"Something...chloroform I think," Hitchens said. "But they took...Alec. I think...God it hurts to think...think they planned to come back for me. Nightmare," he added miserably.

81

"Bloody awful nightmare."

"One more question," said Mrs. Pollifax firmly. "When you used the map for your visioning, Mr. Hitchens, did you feel that Inspector Hao was still alive?"

"Yes," he murmured, and then again, "Bloody awful *nightmare.*"

"Yes indeed," said Robin. "Hang in, old chap, we'll find them both, you know."

Mr. Hitchens blinked at him. "We?"

Robin nodded. "First thing tomorrow if you feel up to it."

"Want to...must...sleep now," said Hitchens, and closed his eyes and slept.

"Looks as if you'll have a roommate for the night," said Robin. "Can you manage?"

"I'd manage better if you'll tell me what's wrong in Hong Kong that brought you here."

Robin glanced at Mr. Hitchens and nodded. "Let's try the bathroom, I'd just as soon he not hear this and I can't be sure he's asleep." Entering first, he said generously, "You can have the edge of the tub."

She laughed and sat down. "All right, I'm perched. Now talk."

"In capsule form?" He glanced at his watch. "It's well past midnight, definitely in capsule form, so try picturing a map with arrows converging on Hong Kong — arrows from Europe, the Middle East and the United States, all pointing to this tiny island in the China Sea."

Mrs. Pollifax said crisply, "The arrows denoting what?"

With equal crispness Robin replied. "Puzzling rumors, coincidences, tips, thefts, the possibility that guns are being smuggled somewhere into the area, and now a man like Inspector Hao mysteriously missing."

"Involving *Hong Kong?*" she said incredulously.

"I know," he said, nodding sympathetically. "A tight little island protected by Britain's Army and Navy, a haven for international money, the commercial hub of the East. Yet behind the scenes here there *is* an active criminal element dealing heavily in narcotics — it's called the Triad — and lately rumors of an explosion of corruption in the police echelons. Inspector Hao just may have learned more than was healthy for him because his disappearance is as mysterious as his abrupt departure from the special force. All we do know for certain is that Hong Kong has become a magnet that's pulling together a number of unrelated incidents in the criminal world, which spells out something violent being planned here."

Frowning over this Mrs. Pollifax said, "Yet as evidence none of this sounds very substantial."

Robin laughed. "My dear Mrs. P., if the evidence were more substantial Interpol would have an army of men here instead of just Marko and myself."

"Marko?"

He grinned. "You don't think the third-richest man in the world travels without a social secretary, do you? You'll have to meet him, except of course he's not really a secretary, he's Marko Constantine, one of Interpol's best, but for the moment he does remarkably well answering my phone and taking messages."

"So you're a sort of reconnaissance, too," she said almost absently. "But those arrows, Robin...I mean how—?"

"Diamonds."

*"Diamonds?"*

He nodded. "Interpol's principal job is narcotics control but the drug syndicates frequently use diamonds to make their payments, so we keep an eye on that, too. Diamonds are small, easy to smuggle from one country to another and far more convenient than currency, as you can imagine. Three months ago, in January and February, there came a sudden rash of diamond thefts and murders: two in New York, three in Antwerp, and four in London. Quite extraordinary, actually."

"Why so extraordinary?"

"Because the diamond industry is very tightly controlled – De Beers and its subsidiaries see to that," explained Robin. "Diamonds are not particularly scarce, and if too many should be unleashed on the market at any one time their prices would plunge and their mystique – which is basically illusion and good advertising – would crumble. Therefore the sudden disappearance of a large number of gems sent quite a shock wave through the market and the industry.

"But it's extraordinary for another reason, too," he continued. "I don't suppose you've ever contemplated how diamonds travel from the mines to their markets?"

"No," said Mrs. Pollifax dryly, "I can't say that I have."

"Well, it's handled in an outrageously casual manner, always has been, and it works. The gems travel by insured mail, by ship, by plane, by courier and by salesmen, and the latter two would shame any secret agent in the way they move around the world, making advance reservations in major hotels, then switching at the last minute to some dive of a rooming house, carrying diamonds in shoe boxes, paper bags, money belts, attaché cases. A very discreet and clever group, and the incidence of thefts has been practically nonexistent, yet inside of six weeks eight salesmen or couriers were murdered – at airports, in hotel rooms, on the street, in their cars. And when it all ended – and it ended as suddenly as it began – nearly eight million dollars' worth of diamonds had been stolen."

"Good heavens," said Mrs. Pollifax, "that's certainly a great deal of tax-free money for *someone!* You feel they were all linked together?"

Robin nodded. "There were definite similarities between the two New York murders and eventually a link with Hong Kong, too, because in March three packages of those stolen diamonds were found in a shipment of narcotics being smuggled into Hong Kong. Landed by boat, actually, on one of the islands. The packets were in the same wrappings in which they'd been stolen, which was certainly very careless of someone!"

"How much were those three packets worth?"

"Nearly two million. One package came from an Antwerp murder, two from New York, again implying connection between them all."

Mrs. Pollifax smiled faintly. "Your evidence grows a shade more substantial, yes."

Robin nodded. "That's what shifted our attention to southeast Asia, where we began picking up other rumors lying around in wait for us. The most alarming one is that we've been

86

told by a reliable informant that some very fancy guns have either passed — or are due to pass — through Sri Lanka on their way to Macao. Macao," he added pointedly, "being only forty miles from Hong Kong."

"*Guns!*" echoed Mrs. Pollifax, startled. "But that changes the picture considerably, Robin!"

He said grimly, "Especially where one of them is rumored to be a multiple rocket launcher called 'Stalin's Organ,' which is very portable, small enough to be carried on the roof of a mini-bus or small boat and its rockets launched from either."

Mrs. Pollifax drew in her breath sharply. "You haven't learned their destination?"

He shook his head. "The silence — the cover-up — is astonishing; we can't pierce it, there are almost no leaks and that's *highly* unusual. Our normal informants have gone mum."

Mrs. Pollifax studied his face and then she said slowly, "You're thinking it's the kind of silence that only eight million dollars' worth of stolen diamonds can buy?"

He gave her an appreciative glance. "You see that. . . Yes, it would take something like that to accomplish this kind of secrecy. Bribes here, bribes there. . . But what keeps me awake nights, frankly, is the feeling that this whole damn thing, whatever it may be, is far more advanced than my superiors believe. Which is why I want very much to locate Inspector Hao, who just may have stumbled across whatever's being planned, and know what's going on." He glanced at his watch and shook his head. "And now it's nearly one o'clock and I think we'd better continue this tomorrow, when I'm hoping your Mr. Hitchens will feel well enough for a trip to the New Territories. What interests me right now" — he stopped and grinned, looking suddenly boyish — "is what your plans are tomorrow. Is there the slightest chance–?" He paused hopefully.

"I thought you'd never ask," said Mrs. Pollifax, beaming at him. "Actually I've nothing pending until ten o'clock tomorrow night."

"Bless you for that," he said, and leaned over and kissed her. "I don't know what it is about you but I seem to recall a certain élan that entered the picture once we joined forces in Switzerland. Interpol can be so deadly serious!"

She laughed. "You surely don't miss being a cat burglar, Robin?"

He grinned. "Occasionally, but then I find entering rooms as I did yours tonight a palliative. Breaking and entering were only mild addictions, you know. Shall we leave our respective bathroom perches?"

"At the moment I can't think of a happier thought," she told him.

Opening the door he added, "Sorry I can't carry Mr. Hitchens off for the night but I'm afraid it would be terribly difficult to explain if I were seen, and even harder to explain than his spending the night with you."

"So long as he doesn't snore," she told him gravely.

Robin grinned. "Hit him if he does, although *not*, of course, on the head, poor chap. Look here, I'll be back in the morning, not *too* bright and early but we can't let Alec Hao's trail grow cold." He opened the door to the hall and peered out. "Looks clear," he said, waved at her and went out, closing the door behind him.

# 6

# TUESDAY

If Mr. Hitchens snored during the night Mrs. Pollifax remained blissfully unaware of it: she was too busy sleeping away two nights of plane travel and a long Monday full of surprises. When she awoke at eight and sat up in bed it was to find that Mr. Hitchens was sitting up too, and staring at her from the chaise longue across the room.

He said with dignity, "I am not accustomed to travel, as you know, or to being hit over the head, or to being chloroformed, either, for that matter."

"No," she said, regarding him with interest.

"I have never in my life had such a head-ache," he went on, his voice trembling a little, "and I have the most dreadful feeling that

I am going to cry."

"Yes," she said, and nodded sympathetically. "What I would suggest then, Mr. Hitchens, is that you get up — very very slowly — and go into the bathroom and stand under a hot shower and cry. While you're doing this I'll dress and call room service, order you some *very* strong coffee, and then you can come out."

"Thank you," he said miserably, and allowed her to help him to his feet, place a shower cap snugly over his bandaged head and lead him into the bathroom.

By the time that Robin joined them she and Mr. Hitchens were sitting companionably by the window with breakfast trays, and Mr. Hitchens had attempted an egg. "He's much better," she told Robin. "He's been telling me that his being psychic is of no help at all in his own life, which seems a great pity, or — quite naturally — he would never have come to Hong Kong."

"Ah, but we're terribly glad you did," Robin said warmly. "Do you feel up to showing Mrs. Pollifax and me that water wheel and hut where you lost Alec Hao yesterday?"

Mr. Hitchens had obviously recovered from his forlorn state because he said dryly, "I won't ask how you came through that door without knocking or using a key, or why Lars Petterson should want to—"

Robin cheerfully interrupted him. "Actually I'm an ex-cat burglar working now for Interpol, and I'm not Lars Petterson at all."

Mr. Hitchens nodded matter-of-factly. "It scarcely matters because I can see that this entire trip is meant to be a Learning Experience for me. Absolutely nothing has made sense so far, and probably nothing will, and now Alec is missing as well as his father and yes, I'm ready to show you where the hut is."

Mrs. Pollifax gave him a warm and congratulatory smile.

"Good chap," said Robin. "Let's go then, shall we? I've got Marko in uniform and a rented limousine waiting at the front entrance for us. We, however, will make our exit by the freight elevator and drive away in a small and inconspicuous Renault. Following that, we'll need directions and instructions from you."

Mr. Hitchens pointed to his jacket. "You'll find a map in the inside pocket, the same one I used for Alec, with the general area circled in pencil."

"You mean you simply looked at a map and said 'there'?"

Mr. Hitchens smiled. "It's a little like dowsing, if you're familiar with the word."

Robin, bringing out the map, nodded. "Yes,

indeed, our neighbor in France had a man come in — a water dowser — to locate a missing well on his property."

"Well, there you are," said Mr. Hitchens and climbed gingerly to his feet, stood a moment steadying himself and smiled. "Amazing! I'm better. Shall we go?"

Mrs. Pollifax decided with some amusement that Mr. Hitchens had reserves and dimensions that were surprising even himself. Certainly the pedantic quality that he'd worn like a coat on the plane was taking second place now to a different Albert Hitchens whose eyes shone with delight as they crept down the hall, descended to the basement in the freight elevator and found their way out into the street to the inconspicuous Renault. "What a remarkable experience," he said. "I feel just like a spy."

Robin gave Mrs. Pollifax an amused glance, brought out a visored cap and dark glasses, took the driver's seat and handed Mrs. Pollifax a map. "I suggest you crouch down out of sight in the back, Mr. Hitchens," he told him, "Mrs. Pollifax being the only one of us who's of no possible interest to surveillants, which is why she can wear brilliant red and pink roses on her hat."

"On the contrary," said Mrs. Pollifax, hastily removing the hat and placing it in her lap, "I was followed all yesterday afternoon after my visit to a curio shop called Feng Imports."

Robin gave her a sharp glance. "When we have a moment I think I'd like to hear—"

"Good God, you too?" gasped Mr. Hitchens from the back seat. "My three wives — if they could only *know!*"

"Three?" echoed Robin, giving Mrs. Pollifax an astonished glance.

"Who all assumed that psychics lived exciting lives and were *deeply* disappointed," she explained.

"Except for Ruthie," called Mr. Hitchens from the floor behind them. "*She* didn't mind my being a dull chap."

"Ruthie we must hear more about," Robin called back to him, "but Hong Kong traffic is fiendish, save it for later."

Mrs. Pollifax decided that she, too, wanted to hear more about Ruthie, but she occupied herself now with tracing their route on the map through traffic that was, as Robin had predicted, fiendish, as drivers jockeyed recklessly for place and slipped in and out among the more sober travelers, their horns bleating a symphony of discordant notes. But they were not being followed, as she pointed out to Robin. "Do you think," she asked him, "that your friend Marko is still waiting at the front entrance with the limousine?"

Robin shook his head. "No, by now he will have telephoned up to our suite – oh, we're very elegant, we have a suite – after which he will have returned to the limousine looking petulant, and swearing noisily at the idle and impulsive rich, and after chatting with the other chauffeurs and asking a large number of interesting questions about who they drive for, he will return the car to the garage."

"Poor Marko," she murmured.

"Don't you believe it," said Robin as they entered the tunnel that would take them under the harbor to Kowloon. "Not too long ago I swabbed decks and pulled nets on a fishing boat in the Mediterranean while Marko did nothing but sit on deck with binoculars, keeping an eye on drug smugglers nosing along the coast. My blisters were monstrous." Emerging from the tunnel he called over his shoulder, "You can come out now, Mr. Hitchens, and just in time to see Hong Kong's newest triumph, Tsim Sha Tsui East, most of it built on land reclaimed from the harbor."

Mr. Hitchens surfaced, and both he and Mrs. Pollifax stared at the enormous complex of hotels, malls, offices and restaurants before they swung into Chong Wan Road, which soon turned into Austin Road, and at last met with

Kowloon's famous Nathan Road, where the oriental and the old triumphed over the new.

"Now that you're visible and accessible," Robin said to Mr. Hitchens, "what exactly did Alec Hao tell you about his father yesterday? You have the advantage of me there because I didn't even know that his son Alec was back in Hong Kong until a few days ago, and by that time he was either not answering the door or the phone, or was never at home."

"He was probably out searching for his father," said Mr. Hitchens. "He told me very little, only that his father had been an inspector in the Hong Kong police department, that his father had grown upset and angry a few weeks ago — something to do with his work — and had suddenly resigned to investigate something important, but he didn't confide in Alec what it was. Then one morning his bed hadn't been slept in, and no one could find him, and three days later Alec cabled and then phoned me in Massachusetts because the police were getting nowhere."

"Keep an eye out for Boundary Street," Robin told Mrs. Pollifax in an aside. "And do the police know that you're here?" he asked Mr. Hitchens.

"Alec didn't say. Our time together," went on Mr. Hitchens, returning to the pedantic, "could be neatly divided into: first, mutual greetings; two, getting down to psychic work, which needed a few hours; three, our travels in the car, and four, our common effort to find the hut once we reached that area."

"How very precise," said Robin weakly.

"And there's Boundary Street," put in Mrs. Pollifax, giving him an understanding smile. "We leave Kowloon now?"

Robin nodded. "Full speed ahead into New Territories, aiming roughly for Yuen Long. Find it on your map?"

"Got it," said Mrs. Pollifax.

Their route lay along a coast road that skirted island-dappled bays on their left and steep mountains on their right, until at Castle Peak Bay they swung north to meet with Hong Kong's farmland. And how lovely it is, thought Mrs. Pollifax, her eyes feasting on a a soft lush green made even more tender by the volcanic texture of the rocky slopes that held it captive on either side. Every inch of the green fields looked manicured, the fields laid out in tidy squares or crescents or rectangles as far as the eye could see, interrupted only by low-slung whitewashed buildings. To her delight she began to see duck ponds, the ducks so brilliant a white in the sunshine they looked as if they'd been freshly laundered before being dropped beside their dazzling blue ponds. It was difficult to remember that violence had been done to Mr. Hitchens and Alec in such a radiant and wholesome setting, she thought. Mr. Hitchens appeared to have forgotten it too as he marveled at two women he saw walking along the road, wearing black hats like huge lampshades with pleated ruffles hanging from them.

"Haaka women," said Robin. "Their being in Hong Kong goes *way* back in time."

"My camera, my camera," mourned Mr. Hitchens, and then, abruptly, he cried, "There it is — over there, see it? The water wheel!"

"Right," said Robin, and braked to a stop.

It lay at a distance of perhaps a quarter of a mile from the road, a very charming wheel set near the edge of a narrow stream of water, surrounded by fields and not far from a copse of green trees.

"The hut's behind the trees," said Mr. Hitchens. "There's no road in, we have to walk."

"So be it," said Robin, and turned off the ignition.

As they climbed out of the car Mrs. Pollifax gave Mr. Hitchens an inquiring glance. "Head hurting?" she asked, for she thought he looked decidedly paler than he'd looked when they left the hotel.

"No," he said. "No, I just feel — uneasy,

that's all." His lips tightened. "I'm all right."

A slender path edged the fields and they entered on it, walking single file, the sun hot now that they'd left the harbor behind them. They didn't speak; something of Mr. Hitchens's uneasiness had transferred itself to both Mrs. Pollifax and Robin, and they walked quickly and in silence. Reaching the water wheel they found a rough board bridge tossed across the irrigation canal; Mrs. Pollifax took the lead and headed for the trees that sheltered the hut, its outlines discernible now.

"Yes, that's the place," Mr. Hitchens said, looking increasingly unhappy.

The hut was roughly twelve feet by fifteen, mysteriously added to this sea of fields and just as mysteriously abandoned. The primitive door creaked and groaned as Mrs. Pollifax pushed it open and she blinked at the sudden darkness inside. The hut was empty, or so she thought until her eyes, adjusting to the dimness, saw the shape of something huddled on the floor in the corner.

And then, "Oh dear God," she said in a strangled voice as she moved closer and saw that it was a man.

Robin was just behind her. "Don't look," he said sharply, and bringing out a pocket flashlight he knelt beside the crumpled body.

But of course she looked, thinking how strange death was and how it ought to be honored, not turned from in dismay just because it was a mystery, an Unknown that could never be solved by human beings bent on solving every Unknown. The light shone on the face of a middle-aged Chinese male, his eyes open in astonishment at something unseen beyond them; he wore a gray silk suit and a white shirt, both of them smudged with dirt. There was a neat small bullet hole over his left eyebrow, with gray powder marks radiating from it; his right hand gripped a gun.

Robin said grimly, standing up, "It's Inspector Hao, and he's dead."

Behind her Mr. Hitchens said, "When?"

Robin knelt again and touched face, wrists and ankles. "Not too long ago. He *was* alive yesterday, you were right about that."

Abruptly Mrs. Pollifax said, "Keep the light on, Robin, there's something, a piece of paper—" She leaned over and removed a slip of white paper from Hao's left hand. Holding it to the light she read aloud, " 'I despair. To be thought guilty—' " She lowered it thoughtfully. "Suicide note?" she suggested with skepticism. "After he's been missing for two weeks?" She handed it to Robin.

Robin studied the note with a frown while

Mr. Hitchens peered at it over his shoulder. "I don't believe in this," he said at last. "A torn fragment addressed to no one at all, the sentence unfinished, no signature and the gun placed in his hand... This has been set up to look like a suicide and I don't believe in it for a minute."

"Murder," said Mrs. Pollifax, naming it, and thought how bizarre the word sounded in this silent, primitive hut built into such a serene landscape.

Mr. Hitchens said, "But the gun, and if that's his handwriting—?"

"Could have been torn from a letter or a diary," pointed out Robin.

Mrs. Pollifax, looking curiously around her, said, "I wonder if he was killed here at all, Robin. There's no breeze this morning. If he was shot only a few hours ago in such close quarters shouldn't there be a lingering smell of gunpowder? And look at the floor."

Robin whistled. "The only footprints are ours — you're right."

The three of them knelt and examined the earthen floor in the light of Robin's pocket flash. "They really made a mistake here," Robin said. "Someone either didn't think ahead, or they panicked, because these tiny swirls and ridges in the dust are the marks of a broom, aren't they? He has to have been killed somewhere else and brought here."

Mr. Hitchens shivered. "I don't like this."

Mrs. Pollifax said tartly, "One has to wonder how on earth they managed to carry him so far, and over that bridge, but in the dark of night I daresay anything's possible." She turned and looked at Inspector Hao's body. "The police can't possibly overlook there being no footprints, can they? I mean, Inspector Hao didn't simply drop through the roof, how can they possibly buy the suicide theory?"

Robin shrugged. "It depends on just who among the police Damien Hao didn't trust, and I'd say it depends, too, on just who *wants* it to be a suicide."

Mrs. Pollifax nodded. "Then it's up to me, Robin, since you're Interpol, and I don't like the way this has been arranged either." She crossed the floor, knelt beside the body and pried loose the gun from Hao's stiffening fingers. "Beretta nine-millimeter Luger," she announced, and dropped it into her purse. Removing the suicide note from Robin's hand with equal dispatch she dropped it, too, into her purse. "I think," she said in a clear firm voice, "that in a situation like this it's kinder to remove all doubt about its being anything but cold-blooded murder."

"Good girl," said Robin with feeling.

Mr. Hitchens looked at her with admiration. "You dared – just like that! But you're right, you know, I feel it. I feared – felt ill – as soon as I saw the hut. But where Alec can be–" His voice trailed away anxiously.

Robin said soberly, "What I don't like is feeling that someone's way ahead of us in knowing what comes next. I think someone *knew* you'd come back here this morning, Mr. Hitchens, giving them an excellent opportunity to arrange Inspector Hao's body here for you to discover and report."

"Then what do you suggest?" asked Hitchens alertly.

"That you very obediently discover and report the body." Robin nodded. "Yes, I think this is where you go public, Mr. Hitchens: U.S. PSYCHIC IN HONG KONG TO FIND MISSING POLICE INSPECTOR – that sort of thing. Just leave us out of it, Mrs. Pollifax and me. You woke up this morning in your own hotel room – after being hit over the head yesterday – and you returned this morning to this hut to look for Alec. You don't even *know* me."

Mr. Hitchens nodded, looking boyish and excited again. "I can do that, yes."

Mrs. Pollifax, watching Robin, said, "You have something in mind for us, I'm thinking?"

He grinned. "You bet. I'll wipe away our footprints now — dragging my jacket across them should do it, although I shudder at the cleaning bill — and after Mr. Hitchens has established his footprints on the floor we'll go back to the car, all of us, and take Mr. Hitchens to a telephone. After that he'll be on his own."

"How did he get here?" put in Mrs. Pollifax quickly.

"Taxi," said Robin, ushering them out into the sunlight and removing his jacket.

"Taxi," repeated Mr. Hitchens. "Never heard of you. . .came alone in a taxi. . ."

"Your turn now," said Robin, emerging from the hut. "Walk inside, discover the body, do a little pacing back and forth and walk out."

Once Mr. Hitchens had complied, still murmuring "Taxi. . .never heard of you. . ." they prepared to leave. But Mrs. Pollifax, the last to go, lingered for just a moment on the threshold of the hut and looked back at the huddled body of Inspector Hao in the corner.

"God bless," she whispered to whatever spirit might be lingering, and silently pledged her help to find his killer and his son.

They left Mr. Hitchens in Yuen Long, where he practiced his new role by thanking them loudly for giving him a ride when he had flagged them down. "But you *will* be looking for Alec now?" he asked in a lower voice, anxiously.

"Yes," promised Robin, "but it's better you not know how or where, because you might let it slip."

As Robin gunned the motor, Mrs. Pollifax leaned forward to call to him, "Leave messages – knock on my door – keep in touch, Mr. Hitchens! Oh dear, he *does* look lonely," she said as Robin turned the car and headed back toward Hong Kong, leaving Mr. Hitchens standing uncertainly beside a stall heaped with vegetables.

"He won't be lonely for long," Robin told her, "he'll shortly be surrounded by police and newspapermen – this is going to be very big news on the island."

"And you and I?"

"We," said Robin, "are going to burgle the Hao residence."

She laughed. "How smoothly things go when one knows a cat burglar! You're amazing, Robin, but won't there be people in the house?"

"He and Alec lived alone," explained Robin. "Wife dead, older daughter married and living in Bangkok, second daughter in college in Europe somewhere, Alec newly graduated from college and back home to job-hunt. The house is off Lion Rock Road in Kowloon and the important thing is to get there before the police."

Mrs. Pollifax nodded. "Hoping, I suppose, that Damien Hao left behind some clue to all this that Alec may have missed...Have you visited the house before?"

"Only to knock — twice as a matter of fact — when no one was at home. I seem to recall a lavish amount of shrubbery for concealing nefarious people like myself but if you'll put that fantastic hat back on your head, dear Mrs. P., it will add a marvelous note of respectability to our mission, because no burglar would ever dare to wear such a hat, believe me."

When they reached the Hao's neighborhood and Robin pointed out their target Mrs. Pollifax saw that he was certainly right about the shrubbery. There was a six-foot wall around the house and the outline of a tile roof nearly hidden by trees, among them, noted Mrs. Pollifax, a mimosa. Robin parked discreetly across the street and they approached the gate in the wall quickly, with the confidence of two people given every right to be there. Four minutes later, following Robin's expertise with a set of delicate lock-picking instruments, they were inside the house.

It was dim inside, the matchstick shades at each window sending alternating lines of sun and shadow across the tile floors. There was a living room, a dining room, a small kitchen and a screened porch in the rear. It looked like any suburban house in America to Mrs. Pollifax, except for a niche in the living room that bore a large gilt Buddha smiling serenely down at their feeble worldly struggles, and at their entrapment in anger, greed and delusion: The Eightfold Path, she remembered with a smile.

"Upstairs," Robin said impatiently. "We need a desk, a study, a safe."

A moment later they had entered Inspector Hao's study at the top of the stairs and were staring at a room swept by chaos: at a steel file cabinet battered open with a sledgehammer, at a desk whose drawers stood open with half their contents strewn across the floor.

"I was afraid of this, damn it," growled Robin. "With Alec out of the way someone had carte blanche here."

*"They,"* echoed Mrs. Pollifax, beginning to feel a presence and wondering if a personality would eventually arrive, too. "Well, whoever they are they were certainly in a hurry. This must be how and where they found that slip of paper to use for a suicide note. What are we looking for?"

"Anything with words written or typed on it — and we're in a hurry, too," said Robin grimly. "You take the desk, I'll take the floor and the two fiiling cabinets."

"Treasure hunt," murmured Mrs. Pollifax, and sat down at the desk to sift what remained in the drawers: a bottle of ink, an abacus, a snapshot album, a few pencils, loose photos and a thick stack of white typing paper.

"Nothing," said Robin angrily, slamming shut the last drawer of the file cabinet. "They took everything of any importance, damn it, and there are only bills on the floor."

Mrs. Pollifax had carefully exhumed the neat pile of typing paper from its drawer; now she gripped the sheets firmly at one corner and waved them back and forth to see if anything had been caught among them. A torn fragment from a newspaper fluttered to the rug, and putting down the sheaf of paper she picked it up and looked at it.

"Good heavens!" she said in a startled voice.

Robin was at her side at once. "What is it?" and then, "Good God!"

It was the photograph of a man that had been roughly torn from a newspaper some time ago, for the newsprint was yellowed with age, and across the top of the clipping someone – undoubtedly Damien Hao – had angrily scrawled WHEN? The man in the news picture faced the camera squarely, as was the custom in prison photos, and there was an identifying prison number across his chest, but no name. The face was wooden, every feature sharpened by the bright lights bent upon it; there were no printed words included with the photo to explain the man but Mrs. Pollifax had recognized him at once. "Robin," she said, "I know this man, but what is he doing in Inspector Hao's desk drawer?"

Robin turned and looked at her strangely. "You mean, of course, that you know who he is."

Mrs. Pollifax shook her head. "No of course not, I mean I just keep running into him."

"Running into him?" Robin gripped her arm, his voice incredulous and urgent. "What do you mean, *running into him?* Where? For God's sake—"

She stared at him in astonishment. "Why, he was on the plane with me from San Francisco — we flew into Hong Kong together, and yesterday morning I saw him in Dragon Alley when I was watching for the young man I was to contact at Feng Imports."

Robin said in a strangled voice, "Plane... Feng Imports...Mrs. Pollifax, I think it's time you tell me exactly what your job is here in Hong Kong. This photo — this man — *this is Eric the Red.*"

A chilly finger of shock touched the base of Mrs. Pollifax's spine. "The terrorist? The head of the Liberation 80's Group? The Cairo assassinations, the French hostage affair?" Her shock moved into horror as she remembered the latter: those endless agonizing days, the miscalculations that culminated in the escape of the Liberation 80's Group and the bloody massacre they left behind...

"Let's get out of here," said Robin fiercely. "Let's get out of here and *talk*. My God, Mrs. Pollifax, if Eric the Red is in Hong Kong—"

He scarcely needed to complete the thought, Mrs. Pollifax had already slammed shut the desk drawers and was reaching for her purse. They fled, not speaking: down the stairs, out of the house and through the garden, into the street and to the car; and just in time, for as they drove away a police car turned into the street and passed them.

Glancing back Mrs. Pollifax saw it come to a stop in front of Damien Hao's home: the inspector's death was now official.

# 7

Robin drove quickly and skillfully toward the tunnel that would return them to Hong Kong, his face set in grim lines and his mind obviously occupied. Mrs. Pollifax was grateful for the silence, for if Robin was considering all the ramifications of Eric the Red's being in Hong Kong, placing these beside the facts he'd already garnered, she in turn was considering the ramifications of a known and dangerous terrorist making his first stop in Hong Kong at Feng Imports...Feng Imports, where Mr. Detwiler was already under suspicion of betraying Carstairs and the Department, where she had not been allowed to see Sheng Ti, where she'd been given a costly Buddha and promptly placed under surveillance.

It was possible, she thought, that her assignment and Robin's assignment were dovetailing, and that a great deal more was going on at Feng

Imports than anyone had guessed.

Robin said abruptly, "We'll go to my rooms, it's time you meet Marko." He leaned over and switched on the car radio and they listened to a crisp male voice announcing the death of Inspector Hao.

"...discovered by Albert Hitchens, an American psychic brought to Hong Kong by Inspector Hao's son, Alec, to find his missing father. Mr. Hitchens had visited the shed yesterday afternoon with Alec Hao, and police are looking into his story that he was assaulted there and Alex Hao kidnapped, leaving Hitchens to find his way back to his hotel alone last evening."

"A new Learning Experience for him," quoted Mrs. Pollifax dryly.

"This morning," continued the voice, "once recovered from the attack, he took a taxi back to the shed to look for Alec Hao and found instead the body of the missing police inspector. Police estimate that Damien Hao's death occurred sometime between 5 a.m. and 7 a.m. this morning. He was shot at close range with a nine-millimeter gun. There is no suggestion of suicide."

"Good — that should startle his killers," put in Robin testily.

"Damien Hao was fifty-five, a member of the..."

Robin snapped off the radio. "And Alec still

112

missing! If it's the Liberation 80's Group that has him—"

"In general," said Mrs. Pollifax in a kind voice, "I think it better not to allow the imagination to take over at moments like this; it drains the energy."

Robin gave her a wan smile. "Experienced, are you?"

"Mildly," she admitted. "Much better to use energy looking for him, because whatever hell he's going through now it's his hell, and we can't manage or change it for him."

"Point well taken," said Robin as he edged the Renault into a parking space at the rear of the hotel. "All right, let's take ourselves to the freight elevator again and have that desperately needed conference, if you please."

"And meet Marko," she added.

"Yes, and meet Marko," he assured her.

Ten minutes later, in the sumptuous suite provided for Lars Petterson, Mrs. Pollifax was meeting Marko Constantine.

"So you are the cupid-playing and fantastic Emily Pollifax of whom I hear," he said, gravely studying her face as he held her hand in a warm grip. "The look of the innocence and of the great earth mother, and the spirit of a boy shinnying down ropes and knowing the karate. *Saluté!*" he murmured, and kissed her hand.

113

Mrs. Pollifax laughed. "But I didn't expect such charm, I wasn't warned! How do you do, Marko."

"The charm is natural, for I am both French and Greek," he announced. "My delight at meeting you is thoroughly authentic — this you must believe — but I think now we get down to very serious business and you will not experience my charm for a long time because I have heard the news, Robin. You both found the body as well as this Mr. Hitchens?"

"Yes, we found Hao dead — and much more," Robin told him grimly.

"Then we talk," said Marko, and gestured Mrs. Pollifax to a nearby chair.

She sat down, both amused and impressed by Marko and glad that he was not an antagonist, for despite his charm she sensed in him the underlying toughness of steel. Outwardly he was small and lithe, a battered little man in his thirties with a radiant smile and a scar on his face that ran from his left cheekbone down to his jaw. His skin was swarthy, his hair black and his dark eyes surprisingly kind, with the wisdom of an old soul. She thought that he looked rather like a monkey, but a most agreeable monkey, for he was attractive — *very* attractive, she decided — in the way that unusual people so often were. He was wearing what must have been his chauffeur's uniform of the morning for he was entirely in black: a silk turtleneck jersey and black slacks, but she saw that he was barefoot as he sprang into a chair and tucked his feet under him.

Robin chose the couch, saying, "We sit and we tell you what we found in Damien Hao's house, which was quietly visited by the two of us after finding Hao dead. And then we hear from Mrs. Pollifax about Feng Imports."

"Feng what?"

Robin pointed to Mrs. Pollifax. *"Her* assignment, Marko, which gives every evidence of wandering into ours, because Eric the Red—"

"Eric the Red!" interrupted Marko. "Mon Dieu...! No, I say frankly, my God!"

"Exactly," Robin agreed and, opening his wallet, he removed the torn news clipping and handed it to Marko, describing how it was found. "At which point, having unearthed it," he said, "Mrs. Pollifax confounded, startled and shocked me by casually announcing that whoever this man was she'd flown into Hong Kong on the same plane with him and had seen him yesterday morning coming out of Feng Imports when she was waiting to make a contact there."

Marko whistled and turned to Mrs. Pollifax. "You must know how incredible this is to us.

You must also know – Robin will have told you – why we are in Hong Kong. You find yourself completely sure this is the same man?"

"Yes," she said simply. "He was very much noticed because I had the misfortune to step on his foot, and later Mr. Hitchens scrutinized him carefully – you can try *him* on the photo, too, when he gets back. The man was traveling on a Canadian passport, by the way."

"You know that also!"

Mrs. Pollifax smiled faintly. "If he had been polite – but he made the mistake of calling attention to himself, a cardinal mistake, I believe, in anyone traveling incognito. He was flawlessly groomed, and I've no doubt his clothes all bore Canadian labels, but he did not like his foot stepped on."

"A leopard and his spots," murmured Marko. "It was believed he was hiding in Eastern Germany but lately rumors have surfaced that he had moved on to Italy."

Mrs. Pollifax said, "But when was he in prison?"

Marko turned to Robin. "It was at least ten years ago, was it not? In West Germany, I believe...He broke out with the help of a woman friend, and of course following that–" He shrugged. "Following that you know the rest, he has left terror behind him in many countries.

116

*Too* many. But please — you say he went at once to this place called Feng Imports?"

"He must have, because he still had his overnight bag with him."

Very softly Marko said, "If this is so it changes everything — *everything!* We know now what — but you will tell us please of this Feng Import shop and why you go there."

Mrs. Pollifax drew a deep breath and plunged into her explanation of why she had come to Hong Kong: she described Carstairs's alarm about Detwiler, how Sheng Ti happened to be known to her and why he was important; she described her visit to Feng Imports and her meeting with Mr. Detwiler and how she was followed afterward and she concluded with her interview of the previous evening with Lotus and a very frightened Sheng Ti.

"Eleven passports — and one of them no doubt Canadian," murmured Robin. "He did say eleven?" When Mrs. Pollifax nodded he said, "And he or Lotus will be contacting you tonight?"

"Yes, at least I assume so. If they can."

Robin and Marko exchanged glances. Marko said, "I think we must immediately go and see this place, don't you? Mrs. Pollifax must lead but not be seen, and I think we bring in — how many men? — to watch this place in case Eric the Red returns to it. But until we have more help I am thinking you will have to lose your secretary." His eyes twinkled at Robin. "Shall you phone or I?"

Robin said, "I will." He rose and walked into another room and closed the door.

"And you," said Marko, rising in one fluid easy motion from his chair, "you are not too tired to show us? Tired from this game we play that sometimes brings violent death?"

"What matters," she said slowly, "is to prevent any more deaths. There's young Alec still missing, and if you're thinking what I am—" She did not finish her sentence, but Marko gave her an appreciative glance.

"Yes," he said, and they sat quietly until Robin reappeared.

"There'll be two men here by nine tonight — Krugg and Upshot," he told them, "and a third man — Witkowski — before morning. It's all they can spare at the moment but at least they begin to understand that things are beginning to happen here."

Marko nodded. "Good. I will go and pack my knapsack then, and take over until nine."

"Interpol, but still no local police?" commented Mrs. Pollifax as she placed her hat on her head and skewered it into place with a hatpin.

"I have to remind you that Damien Hao avoided them," Robin said dryly, "and don't forget all those stolen diamonds, which — if they went into bribes — bought a hell of a lot of people. A little paranoia helps in this job, as you know. I'd guess that most of the police here are as trustworthy as you and I, but if Hao *was* framed, and *was* murdered for what he learned, just how do we find which ones can be trusted? It's too chancy just now, like Russian roulette. My superiors are sending in men from Tokyo and Bangkok."

"And what is Marko packing?" she asked quietly.

"Food, radio transmitter, batteries, camera and film and probably a gun. Or so I'd guess. We'll hope like hell we can find a hiding place for him in your Dragon Alley."

Mrs. Pollifax felt a stir of excitement; her watch told her that it was almost two o'clock in the afternoon and that once again she would be missing lunch, but she felt that a missed lunch was a very small price to pay to watch two professionals at work. "I'm ready," she said as Marko emerged from the next room with his knapsack. "We're off to the freight elevator again?"

The first lesson that Mrs. Pollifax learned in

the art of reconnaissance was that there would be no setting foot in Dragon Alley at all. They circled it instead, researching first the street in back of Feng Imports, stumbling through yards and over piles of junk until Mrs. Pollifax finally spotted the high slanted window of Mr. Detwiler's rear workroom, whereupon Robin jotted down location and description in a notebook and stared with particular interest at what looked to be an empty warehouse room on the top floor of a nearby building.

They next moved to the lane on the other side of Dragon Alley and scouted the shop from this approach, squeezing through narrow apertures in a fence and peering around trees until they located the building that faced the front door of Feng Imports. This proved to be a rooming house, a ramshackle wooden affair listing subtly toward the street below. The proprietor of the rooming house was not on the premises, and Mrs. Pollifax was enchanted by the dispatch with which Marko and Robin dealt with this problem: they simply entered the building by the back door and walked up and down halls knocking on doors until they found someone at home.

Their discovery was a man named Pi and they had interrupted his sleep. He slept, he said, because he had lost his job a week ago, and who were they? Over his shoulder Mrs. Pollifax looked into the cubicle he occupied and saw that not only did it have a window, but that the window looked out on Dragon Alley and directly down at Feng Imports. Twenty minutes later Pi had bundled up his belongings — they made a pile no larger than Marko's knapsack — and had sublet his cubicle to them for a week. From the amount of money that was paid to him for both his silence and his absence Mrs. Pollifax thought that he could very well afford to move into the Hong Kong Hilton but Robin and Marko had their stakeout. Once he had gone she and Robin lingered only briefly to help Marko rearrange the furniture, to lay out his lunch — Mrs. Pollifax tried not to regard it too wistfully — and to set up his radio; then they too left.

"What now?" asked Mrs. Pollifax, intrigued by the thought of more revelations.

"Now I'll drop you off at the hotel," Robin said deflatingly, "because I've got to go back and see about renting that second-floor space overlooking the rear of Feng Imports, and for that I'll need some fake business cards that I don't have with me, and a change of outfit. After that I'll set up the radio in our hotel suite and establish contact with Marko. What I hope you'll do is find Mr. Hitchens for me and set up some kind of appointment. I'd like very much to have him verify the news photo of Eric the Red, but also" — Robin gave her a sheepish glance — "also..."

She smiled. "You want to borrow his psychic talents. The only problem may be that with all the publicity he's suddenly getting we may have to stand in line."

Robin swung the Renault into a parking space at the mall entrance to the hotel. "Nonsense," he said. "If that's the case you must gently but firmly remind him of who gave him sanctuary last night in his moment of travail, and just who called a doctor for him, and you might throw in the hint of a terrorist or two and remind him that you and I are on the side of justice, peace and order, etcetera — relatively speaking — and then pray hard that he can answer Inspector Hao's WHEN? We desperately need a date...a week, a month, a day."

"That's a tall order," pointed out Mrs. Pollifax.

"All orders are tall in this business," said Robin, "and at the moment I'm feeling very short." He reached over and opened the door for her. "It's already midafternoon, there's no telling when Hitchens will turn up and I've a great deal to do; we'd better settle for a very firm date early tomorrow morning. I'm a reasonable man," he added. "Offer Mr. Hitchens a luxurious breakfast with us in my suite at eight o'clock. He's just mislaid his employer and he could be wondering where his next meal's coming from."

"I wish I'd thought of that," she said warmly. "Robin, you *are* nice."

He grinned. "Of course I'm nice...If anything comes up, I'll be manning the radio until it's time to meet planes at the airport tonight. See you!" He saluted and drove away to find a parking space and to undoubtedly make his entrance by way of the freight elevator, on which he was becoming a regular commuter. Mrs. Pollifax entered the hotel through the mall to begin a search for Mr. Hitchens.

But she was thinking as she walked through the mall that she would still have no news of Alec to give Mr. Hitchens, and this would be one of the first questions he would ask of her because Alec was the reason for his being in Hong Kong, just as Detwiler was *her* reason for being here. On the heels of this thought came the realization that she'd not thought very much about Detwiler at all today. She had been concerned with Mr. Hitchens and the missing Alec; she had helped discover a body and the identity of the man with the violent aura, and she'd enjoyed very much observing how Robin and Marko set up the surveillance point from which they'd watch Feng Imports, but she'd scarcely given a thought to either Detwiler or Sheng Ti, and they were both her immediate assignment.

She paused to glance idly over the jackets of magazines in one of the shops but they all seemed to have names like *Peek, Spy, Prowl* and *See.* She thought, *If there's a connection between Mr. Detwiler and Eric the Red — and Alec still mysteriously missing — isn't it possible that Detwiler might be hiding Alec in his home, wherever it might be?* She wondered if Detwiler lived in an apartment or a house, and where she could find the nearest phone directory to see if he were listed. Leaving magazines behind, she headed for the escalator to the lobby.

She had just found Detwiler's address and was copying it into her memo pad when she felt herself tapped on the shoulder and Mr. Hitchens said, "I've been looking for you!"

She turned to find herself face to face with a Mr. Hitchens whose face had almost vanished under a huge hat that looked like a cross between a panama and a Stetson. Repressing an urgent impulse to laugh she said in amusement, "Are you in disguise, Mr. Hitchens?"

He said reproachfully, "No, I've an ice pack on my head and it didn't seem quite the thing to wear in the lobby while I waited for you so the manager very kindly loaned me his hat. Shall we sit down?"

"Yes, do let's," she said heartily, and they moved toward the nearest couch.

"I can't tell you how wonderful they've been to me here," he confided. "I've been given another room because apparently I put up quite a fight last night with that — that *thug*, and the maid found my room a shambles this morning. I'm in room 302 now, and" — he paused for breath, beaming at her happily — "and I'm going to be on the television news tonight, it's already taped, and just look—" He held out his newspaper to her. "Fresh off the press!"

They established themselves on the couch, and Mrs. Pollifax unfurled the paper to gaze at a photograph of two policemen and Mr. Hitchens blinking in the sun. Lower on the page was a large close-up of Mr. Hitchens, his bandage at a slightly rakish angle, and a smaller-case headline that read NOTED AMERICAN PSYCHIC IN HONG KONG.

"I'm noted," said Mr. Hitchens happily.

"What fun," she said. "You occupy most of the front page, too, I'm delighted for you, but how are you feeling, Mr. Hitchens? Your wound, I mean."

His hands groped toward his head. "The ice

seems to have melted now. It was just fatigue, I'm sure, but my head had begun to throb." He removed the hat and the ice bag dropped into his lap. Picking it up he said, "You wouldn't have room for this in your purse, would you?"

"No," she said calmly, "I'm already carrying a Beretta pistol and a suicide note and there's no room for an ice bag."

Nodding philosophically he tucked it into his pocket. "But you've not found Alec?"

"Unfortunately not yet," she said, and they both fell silent as a gorgeously robed and be-jeweled man entered the lobby, followed by a retinue of equally as exotic personages, moved across the lobby to the elevators and were whisked out of sight.

"Squantum was never like this," said Mr. Hitchens with a shake of his head.

"Squantum?"

"Where I live, near Boston, but what about Alec?"

"We didn't find him but we found a number of highly interesting clues," said Mrs. Pollifax, "and Robin wants us both to have breakfast with him in his suite tomorrow at eight o'clock to talk about possibilities."

Mr. Hitchens looked pleased.

"He also wants you to look at a photograph, and to—" She paused, seeing that Mr. Hitchens's gaze was now on a tour group that had entered the lobby, a group of tired-looking Americans led by a young Chinese woman with an insignia on her jacket. What startled Mrs. Pollifax was that Mr. Hitchens's jaw was slowly dropping and his eyes widening in astonishment.

"What is it?" asked Mrs. Pollifax.

Mr. Hitchens closed his mouth with a snap. "I don't believe it," he said, and then, "I don't believe it!" A smile spread slowly across his face. "It's Ruthie," he said, and stood up and called out her name.

A woman in the group turned, peered across the lobby, saw Mr. Hitchens and looked as astonished as he had looked a moment ago. Detaching herself from the others, she took a few hesitant steps toward him, stopped, then hurried on to be met in midlobby by Mr. Hitchens, who gave her a shy embrace. Their approaches implied a difficult parting long ago, and a certain amount of uncertainty about meeting.

Mrs. Pollifax smiled as she watched. Ruthie, she remembered, was the wife who had never expected Mr. Hitchens to live an exciting life. His first wife, he had told her, was a kindergarten teacher, his second an aspiring young actress, and his third wife an aspiring young magician. Ruthie, she felt instinctively, was the first wife because no show-business aspirant would ever conceal her personality so firmly behind character. Ruthie was small, and at first glance plain, but at second glance there was an arresting piquant quality about her plainness; her nose, for instance, had an interesting upturn and her chin, though small, was stubborn, and her brown eyes almost too large for her face. She was wearing a brown suit and sensible shoes and she was nearing forty: a nice little brown sparrow of a woman, thought Mrs. Pollifax, smiling at the sensible and practical manner in which she was meeting her former husband. Only the suddenly flushed face betrayed her pleasure at seeing him.

"But I don't understand," Mrs. Pollifax heard her saying. "What are you doing in Hong Kong of all places?"

Mr. Hitchens turned eagerly toward Mrs. Pollifax. "She's here on a tour," he called. "It's Ruthie!"

Ruthie turned quickly to follow his glance, and Mrs. Pollifax recognized the sudden fear in her eyes as she searched for the person to whom Mr. Hitchens was speaking. *She still loves him,* thought Mrs. Pollifax; *is she expecting another young actress or magician?* For Mrs. Pollifax was already writing the scenario of their last parting, and was waiting only to discover if it was accurate.

Ruthie's glance softened as she saw Mrs. Pollifax. "Oh," she said. "Oh!"

Mrs. Pollifax smiled on her with warm understanding. "The reasons for Mr. Hitchens being here," she said, leaving the couch to join them, "are so intricate — I'm Emily Pollifax, by the way — and he has become so embroiled that why don't you just show her the newspaper, Mr. Hitchens?"

The flush on Ruthie's face had subsided; now it burgeoned again as Mr. Hitchens unfolded his newspaper and showed her the photographs on the front page. "Police business," he explained. "Ruthie, you're looking absolutely lovely!"

"And I," said Mrs. Pollifax firmly, "have another errand to do and so I will excuse myself and leave you both to enjoy the rest of the afternoon together."

Ruthie said breathlessly, "Oh no — that is, you mustn't think — I'm on a tour, you know, and we're kept very busy, for instance tonight we visit Hong Kong's nightclubs and—"

Mr. Hitchens, regarding her with pleasure, said "But why not see Hong Kong's night life with *me* tonight, Ruthie?"

At this point Mrs. Pollifax withdrew, leaving

them to the pitfalls and delights of reunion, and escaped to room 614 to find quieter clothes for a reconnaissance trip all her own.

# 8

Once in her room Mrs. Pollifax exchanged her dress for a plain cotton skirt, striped shirt and sandals, and tied a blue-striped scarf around her head. Following this she dug into her suitcase for the hard-cover notebook she always carried with her. Tearing out its first page — into which she'd copied data on the birds at the Zoological Garden for Cyrus — she critically inspected the remaining unlined pages until, nodding with satisfaction, she cut some twenty sheets from their binder and slid them into her purse. Leaving her room she visited the mall again, where she bought a professional-looking clipboard. Then she headed for the main exit where she captured a taxi and gave the driver the name of the street on which Mr. Detwiler lived, but not the precise number.

A surprise soon awaited her: on an island where space was at a premium Mr. Detwiler lived at the base of Victoria Peak in what was obviously a prime residential area, on a pleasant, tree-shaded street where space was of no concern at all, and well-manicured lawns stood between each house. Mrs. Pollifax paid her fare, thanked the driver and stood looking around her, wishing she'd worn her dress and hat after all. Casually she strolled up the street past number 3216 with its discreet sign planted among the shrubs: 3216 — DETWILER — JASMINE HOUSE.

"Small but elegant," she murmured, and comparing it with his shop in the central district, so modest in size and placed in such an out-of-the-way corner, she reminded herself that he did, after all, deal in diamonds. With a sigh she thought, *In for a penny, in for a pound, Emily. Courage!* and continuing past his house she turned in at number 3218 — THE FINCH-BERTRAMS — THE BEECHES.

A maid answered her ring, a little Chinese woman in a voluminous apron. "Good afternoon," said Mrs. Pollifax pleasantly, "I'm taking an advertising survey on how many hours of television you watch each day?"

The woman looked blank. Behind her a clipped English voice called, "Who is it, Ming?" and a chic young woman appeared, looked Mrs. Pollifax over carefully, shrugged and invited her inside.

"Why not?" she said. "My husband won't be home for hours, Ming speaks no English and my God it gets boring in this place."

Some thirty-five minutes later Mrs. Pollifax wrenched herself free, having learned rather too much about Mrs. Finch-Bertram, about her bridge games and her shopping, how little she saw of her husband and of how when she did see him he was either on the telephone all evening or they were entertaining clients at the club. Mrs. Finch-Bertram's attention apparently did not include her neighbor at number 3216; she did, however, watch television and Mrs. Pollifax carefully noted down her replies: soap operas when she was at home, "although of course they're too boring for words," and anything suspenseful "where I can see what clothes they're wearing these days." The problem with being a listener, thought Mrs. Pollifax as she achieved the street again, was that one became such a repository of unsolicited information, and in this case the wrong sort for her purposes.

She had much better luck across the street at number 3217 – THE WONGS; the door was opened by a stunning young Chinese mother wearing blue jeans, her three children lurking behind her and giggling through the entire interview.

"Television? Oh it's my baby-sitter," Mrs. Wong told her with a laugh. "You've hit the right house, it's on constantly, I bless RTV every day."

Mercifully Mrs. Pollifax was not invited inside, and after scribbling down Mrs. Wong's answers to her mythical survey, she asked brightly, "And the house just across the street, are there children at number 3216?"

Mrs. Wong shook her head. "Oh no, that's Tom Detwiler, he's a bachelor. Haven't seen him around for ages but his housekeeper watches TV, I'm sure."

A bachelor...a housekeeper...Mrs. Pollifax thanked her profusely, gave the children a last cheerful wave and decided to proceed directly to Detwiler's house before meeting another Mrs. Finch-Bertram. Crossing the road she looked at the house with an eye this time for convenient corners in which to hide the very inconvenient son of a murdered police inspector. There was, for instance, a large garage at the end of the drive, with rooms above it. The house itself gave the impression of being small but on closer inspection Mrs. Pollifax noticed an added wing that had been rendered invisible from the street by trees. Its architecture was a sophisticated blend of European

134

and oriental: a blue-tile roof that curved upward at each corner in the best Chinese style
but below the roof the structure was sleekly
contemporary, with discreet touches of stone
and teak, and at the front door a massive brass
knob in the shape of a dolphin. She rang and
waited, hoping that Mr. Detwiler hadn't been
seized by an overwhelming impulse to dash
back to his house at this hour, and that his
housekeeper might be cherishing as many
grievances as Mrs. Finch-Bertram to pour into
a listening ear.

As it turned out, his housekeeper had only
one grievance, and a very unexpected one, but
for another voice and a listening ear she had a
real need; Mrs. Pollifax had no sooner announced her advertising survey than she was
urged to come in and do her survey in the
kitchen over a good cup of tea.

"For I get that lonesome," she told Mrs. Pollifax with a shake of her head. "O'Malley's
my name, by the way, Jane O'Malley...and if
it wasn't for me soaps I don't know but what
I'd hand in me notice, even though Mr. Detwiler pays me the moon, nothing stingy about
'im at all, but still if he don't come home soon—!"
She led the way into the kitchen, poured tea
for Mrs. Pollifax in a charming Haviland cup,
and sat down opposite her at the table.

Somewhat confused by this statement Mrs. Pollifax shook her head sympathetically, her voice subtly changing. "Alone all day? I suppose that means leaving dinner for the family on the stove instead of serving it decently."

"Family!" exclaimed Mrs. O'Malley. "There's only him and no dinner at all, for he's not been to home for two months now."

"Not been to—" Mrs. Pollifax stopped and began again. "Oh yes, you *must* get lonesome, I can see that." Was she serious, Mrs. Pollifax wondered: not at home for *two months...?*

Mrs. O'Malley nodded. "Yes, and being here twenty-four hours of the day, too — I've an apartment over the garage, all very shipshape — there's some as would say 'Oh, what an easy time for you' but who's to cook for? A woman likes to have a man to cook for."

"And a fine cook I'm sure you are," said Mrs. Pollifax, nodding.

"I am, yes, me husband said I was the best, Lor' love 'im — British Army he was, and us here so long I couldn't ever go back to England, it's not me home any more, and Mr. Detwiler, he's ever so pleased with my dinner parties — when he gives 'em — for I've taken up gourmet, don't you know."

It was becoming a very real effort for Mrs. Pollifax to hide her astonishment over Mr.

Detwiler's absence from his home but she managed to say soothingly, "Away on a business trip, is he?"

An odd expression came over Mrs. O'Malley's round, honest face — puzzled, thought Mrs. Pollifax, reaching for a word to describe it. "*Some* sort of business," she said, "although once a week comes his laundry to be done, brought by a delivery boy without a word of where he is, and back I send his clean shirts, just the right amount of starch as he likes, but what I say is, it's downright depressing when once there was dinner parties — two, three times a week — and he had his lady friends too, he did. Very lively place it was until two months ago, and now only the errand boy once a week, and me TV for company. So if you're doing a survey you can put me down for lots of telly-watching because otherwise I'd be talking to meself from dawn to dusk."

*Two months,* Mrs. Pollifax was repeating to herself dazedly — how very extraordinary — and hadn't Bishop told her that it was two months ago that Detwiler's reports to the Department had become deceptive and misleading? Aloud she said warmly, "Oh yes, I can see that," and, placing her clipboard on the table and bringing out her pen, she added with a smile, "Like Mrs. Wong across the street, who tells me that she too has her — uh — telly on all day."

Mrs. O'Malley's face softened. "Now she's a dear little thing, and so much happier now her father-in-law's dead." She shook her head. "Such a Nationalist he was — talk talk talk — and she so patient!"

"Nationalist?"

"You know — what China was before the Reds took over, that general Whatsisname — Chiang Kai Shek — who moved his government to Taiwan and always schemed to get back to the mainland." Seeing Mrs. Pollifax's surprise, she explained in a kind voice, "No doubt it seems a long time ago to you, dear — all that happening — but not here in Hong Kong. You have to remember most of the refugees came here running away from the Communists, so there's still feelings about it, like old Mr. Wong across the street flying his Nationalist flag every day on the lawn. Glad to see *that* gone, I can tell you! Now what was you going to ask me?"

Mrs. Pollifax began her survey, Mrs. O'Malley giving her a running commentary on each of her preferred shows, and conscientiously recorded her dawn-to-midnight viewing.

"Widow, too?" asked Mrs. O'Malley, watching her put away her clipboard and pen.

138

Mrs. Pollifax temporarily erased Cyrus from her thoughts and said that yes, she'd been a widow for many years.

Mrs. O'Malley nodded. "And this 'ere inflation — *I* know! What it does to pensions... where you living, dear?"

"Off Lion Rock Road," said Mrs. Pollifax, adopting Inspector Hao's house, and then with a glance at her watch, "but I really must be running along now, I've ever so many more people to see, and it's getting on for five, and—"

"Run you ragged, do they," Mrs. O'Malley said, nodding. "Get yourself a nice housekeepin' job, dear, it's like having your own home, I say."

Mrs. Pollifax laughed as she rose from the table. "Yes, except when your employer goes away for weeks at a time."

"Well, stop in tomorrow if you're doing any surveying in the neighborhood," said Mrs. O'Malley as they reached the front door. "What did you say your name was, dear?"

Mrs. Pollifax felt her mind go blank. "Blank — Irma Blank," she stammered, and fled.

But her visit to Mr. Detwiler's house had produced a shock that she wrestled with strenuously all the way back to the hotel, and in her room once she arrived there, for certainly Mr. Detwiler was not away from Hong Kong on a business trip when she'd spoken with him only yesterday at Feng Imports. Yet he'd not visited his home for two months, and the nagging question to which she found no immediate answer was, *why?*

She tried to remember what she'd prepared herself to find on her visit to his house: something sinister, of course, or she wouldn't have kept the Beretta pistol in her purse when she left the hotel. She found it difficult now to reconstruct in her mind the picture she'd conceived of an attic or outbuilding where Detwiler might have hidden Alec after murdering his father. What she'd found instead was an elegant suburban villa, a devoted housekeeper, and as for Mrs. O'Malley, she couldn't help feeling that if Alec had been on the premises she would have kept him in the kitchen with her for long chats over cups of tea.

She thought, *I'm missing something here...* I've got to stop writing scenarios and free my thoughts for looking at what I've not seen yet...

At ten o'clock that evening Mrs. Pollifax was once again riding through the streets of Hong Kong for a second clandestine meeting with Sheng Ti, but this time Robin was with her.

They had met in the freight elevator as she

left the hotel. "One meets the most distinguished people here," Robin quipped as the doors slid open at basement level and she found herself face to face with him. "Where are you off to now, dear Mrs. P.?"

She told him quickly, "Lotus has called, I'm off to Dragon Alley — in a hurry — she's bribed her roommates again for half an hour."

Robin at once grasped her by the arm. "I'll take you," he said. "The Renault's just outside and I'd like very much to meet this young man of yours."

'You've been to the airport?"

He opened the car door for her. "Yes, and delivered both Interpol men to Marko. Krugg will take over in Dragon Alley from Marko, and then Marko was to deliver Upshot to the street behind, after which he'll be returning to the hotel to eat and sleep. According to Marko nothing's happened except that Sheng Ti left the shop around five-thirty carrying two packages wrapped in brown paper, and came back empty-handed at seven, and I wouldn't mind at all finding out what he was delivering."

"And I," said Mrs. Pollifax, "intend to ask Sheng Ti where Mr. Detwiler is living." She proceeded to tell him of her advertising survey of late afternoon.

"You *have* been busy," he said, giving her an

appreciative glance. "Whatever made you think of doing that?"

"Remembering that Detwiler is my assignment," she said promptly.

"He is, isn't he," mused Robin with some surprise.

She smiled. "I have also — besides writing Cyrus a letter and doing my Yoga — watched Mr. Hitchens on the evening TV newscast. I thought he did a very sophisticated job, handling questions, and there wasn't the faintest suggestion of his knowing anyone in Hong Kong except Alec Hao."

"Good for him, I'm relieved."

"And," she added triumphantly, "you may not have had time to pick up the late edition of the newspaper but there's a photo of Alec Hao on the first page, with the headline, HAS ANYONE SEEN HIM? I'm carrying it with me to show Lotus and Sheng Ti."

"I marvel," said Robin with a twinkle. "You insist with rare talent on sticking to the basics, or what do you call it, the nitty-gritty?"

She said frankly, "Well, I don't want you to forget Alec. I quite understand how you might, what with Eric the Red entering the picture, but Mr. Hitchens is very concerned about him. I've seen Mr. Hitchens, by the way, and he'll join us for breakfast in the morning at eight —

he sounded delighted — and of course he knows nothing about terrorists, he's still rooted in yesterday and losing Alec."

"Yesterday...when we were all a shade more innocent — and why do I feel I'm being properly reproached and chastised, and making Mr. Hitchens desperately unhappy?"

She laughed. "Well — not *too* unhappy, because—" She told him about Ruthie and it was his turn to laugh.

"The manifestations of fate!" he exclaimed. "And she's on one of those awesome tours that pass through countries in this season? I'd like to meet her, I'm curious."

Mrs. Pollifax nodded. "I think you'd like her, she's not a beauty like Court—"

"No one's like Court," said Robin firmly.

Amused, Mrs. Pollifax said, "No, of course not — for you at least — but for Mr. Hitchens — well, I'm going to be very interested in finding out just what happened between him and Ruthie, because she strikes me as a very sensitive and sensible person and I must say his reaction was that of a man experiencing a small miracle." She added quickly, "There's a parking space up ahead on the right."

Robin slid the Renault into it with skill. "Thanks. A common miracle or a divine one?"

She smiled. "No miracle is ordinary, but any

woman who appreciates green bananas and television reruns — as Mr. Hitchens does — certainly could be a divine miracle. We've two blocks to walk now, we turn at the corner with the sign JAZZ NITELY. GIRLS."

Opening the creaky gate and entering the tiny compound at number 40 Dragon Alley, Mrs. Pollifax found Lotus waiting again in the shadows. Seeing that she was not alone Lotus stood up, ready to flee, her face distressed.

"A friend," she told Lotus. "Good friend, too, it's all right, believe me."

Lotus gave Robin a doubtful glance, but she led them through the entry and into the dim room that Mrs. Pollifax had visited before.

"Good God, looks like an opium den," murmured Robin, entering behind her.

To Mrs. Pollifax's surprise, Sheng Ti accepted Robin's presence at once, which she found touching until she realized that it implied a complete and unquestioning trust in her that she found alarming. "Friend," said Sheng Ti, shaking Robin's hand and beaming. "New friend. Pliss — a seat."

They sat down under the smoking lamp, their faces orange in its weird light, and Mrs. Pollifax began their conference by unwrapping a napkin full of sweet buns and placing them on the table. Beside them she laid twenty Hong

Kong dollars. "For renting the room for half an hour," she told Lotus. "Now to business! Did you do errands today for Mr. Detwiler, Sheng Ti?"

He nodded. "Yes, and I show memory for you." Closing his eyes he recited, "Two packages diamonds: one to Donald Chang, Nga Tsin Wai Road, apartment near airport Kowloon, and other to post office, one package *insured*, Gem Mart, Bombay, India." He opened his eyes and smiled.

"The Hong Kong address particularly interests me," said Robin, "but I note both with thanks. Can you fill in the address for me of Donald Chang?"

Sheng Ti nodded, and bringing out a slip of paper read off the number of both the street and the apartment. "I work good?" he asked Mrs. Pollifax eagerly.

She smiled. "You 'work good,' yes." She brought out Alec Hao's picture in the newspaper. "Now have you seen *this* man at Feng Imports?"

"Not there, no," he said, shaking his head.

"You mean you've seen him elsewhere?" gasped Mrs. Pollifax.

He pointed at the picture. "In newspaper this night, yes; I study paper every night in shop to learn English."

Mrs. Pollifax's heart sank. "I see. And Lotus — you?"

"No, never," Lotus told her.

"Then what about this man?" she asked, bringing out the worn newspaper photo of Eric the Red. "Do either of you recognize *him* from the shop?"

"No," said Lotus, and Mrs. Pollifax remembered that she'd not yet arrived at the shop when the man with the violent aura made his exit.

Sheng Ti, however, narrowed his eyes as he studied the picture and suddenly nodded vigorously. "Yes — he come very early, yesterday I think, yes. I was packing *yudě —*"

"Jade," explained Lotus.

"*Shi,* jade . . . and when he come in I am sent away fast to buy *qishui.*"

"Soft drinks," put in Lotus.

Sheng Ti nodded impatiently. "But I see him anyway as I go. He had — funny marks on —" He touched his cheek with his fingers. "This man very same."

"Yes," said Mrs. Pollifax, nodding.

Robin leaned forward, his voice harsh. "Have you seen him again? Do you know where he went? Did you hear what name he was called?"

Sheng Ti sadly shook his head.

"One other question," said Mrs. Pollifax,

"and do have a sweet bun."

"Su-eet boon?"

"Yes. Where does Mr. Detwiler sleep? Does he stay at the shop? Does he live there now?"

Sheng Ti looked at her blankly. "I leave eight, nine, ten o'clock, him still there, *Xiānsbeng,* I not know."

"Good heavens," murmured Robin, "and what time do you begin work?"

Sheng Ti shrugged. "Six sometimes, maybe eight."

Robin whistled. "Slave labor!"

"Lotus?" asked Mrs. Pollifax.

The girl frowned, puzzled. "I hadn't thought of it before, but for weeks now Mr. Detwiler's been at the shop when I leave at six. This is not usual, he always used to leave at five or half-past, for he has a house—"

"Yes," said Mrs. Pollifax. "Where does Mr. Feng live?"

Her brow cleared. "Oh, he has rooms over the shop."

Mrs. Pollifax met Robin's questioning glance with triumph. Rooms over the shop . . . Detwiler could be staying with Feng, then, to remain in charge, to be available for any decision. Mrs. O'Malley, she thought, would not be seeing Detwiler, then, until whatever he planned was completed.

Whatever he planned...She sighed: to learn that Detwiler was remaining downtown nights was not a very large thing to learn but she was nevertheless glad to place his whereabouts at night.

"Something wrong?" Sheng Ti asked anxiously.

Robin said thoughtfully, "Are either of you aware of a radio transmitter on the premises?"

Lotus said, "There is a music radio...*shou-yinji,*" she explained to Sheng Ti. "What is upstairs I do not know but I think two rooms. What is it?" she asked.

Mrs. Pollifax glanced at Robin, who imperceptibly shook his head. "It's better you don't know, not yet," she told them both, "but it's terribly important, and this man" — she pointed to the picture of Eric the Red — "this man is very dangerous, a bad one. If he comes again to Feng Imports or if you hear anything about him, let us know at once, will you?"

"Him too?" asked Lotus, glancing at Robin.

"Him too," Mrs. Pollifax assured her gravely.

Robin was already jotting down his number. "Someone will be at this telephone if you can't reach Mrs. Pollifax."

"Or come to the hotel if it's important," said Mrs. Pollifax, and removing another twenty Hong Kong dollars from her purse she gave Lotus ten and Sheng Ti ten. "For taxi."

"So much money," murmured Sheng Ti in awe. "And su-eet boons, too. We call ten tomorrow again?"

"Please do," she said, and as Robin stood up she rose to shake hands warmly with Sheng Ti and Lotus. "Thank you both," she told them, and they left.

"I like your young man," Robin said as they drove back to the hotel through streets brilliant with flashing neon. "He's badly frightened, though."

"Yes," she said, and then, "I am, too, aren't you?"

This time only Robin used the freight elevator; Mrs. Pollifax, wondering if there were any cables from Carstairs, stopped at the desk in the lobby to inquire; there was indeed a cable for Mrs. Reed-Pollifax and she carried it unopened up to her room, thinking how long a day it had been. It had begun with Mr. Hitchens asleep on her chaise longue, after which they had found the body of Inspector Hao; she and Robin had discovered the identity of the man with the black aura; she had observed stakeouts at Feng Imports, done her advertising survey and had seen Sheng Ti and Lotus again. It was no wonder that she was feeling drained and tired.

She placed her purse next to the figure of the Buddha that stood on the bureau, the expression on its face one of an unbelievable serenity that at this moment Mrs. Pollifax envied with all her heart. With a sigh she slit open the envelope of the cable to discover that it was not from Carstairs but from Cyrus. She read: RAINED OUT STOP RETURNED EARLY STOP CATCHING FIRST PLANE TO JOIN YOU THURSDAY NIGHT HONG KONG TIME STOP MISS YOU SEE YOU LOVE YOU CYRUS.

Mrs. Pollifax read it over a second time, feeling all of her tiredness drop away from her like an outworn coat. Cyrus was coming... *Cyrus!*

She laughed with delight, and catching the eye of the Buddha she thought for a moment that it smiled back at her; she made it a very small, whimsical curtsy before she turned out the lights.

# 9

# WEDNESDAY

Mrs. Pollifax drifted in and out of an uneasy dream, and – waking – opened her eyes, found it still night, and closed them again, wondering why there persisted a feeling of something wrong. With her eyes still closed she sent her mind's antenna out to probe: it wasn't Cyrus, who was on his way to Hong Kong now, nor was it – her thoughts froze as she heard the faintest whispering sound of motion nearby. What was wrong, she realized, was here and now, and in this room.

She was not alone.

Mrs. Pollifax opened her eyes and cautiously turned her head to that she could observe the room. The heavy drapes had not been completely drawn across the window, and a dim

151

and eerie light from the street spilled across the floor. In the center of the room stood a man, his outline clearly discernible against the lighter patch of window. He was standing very still and Mrs. Pollifax at once recognized that stance, having experienced it herself: in her sleep she must have turned over restlessly, or called out, and he had frozen, waiting for her to settle back again into sleep.

Mrs. Pollifax had no intention of settling into sleep, however. Through half-closed eyes she waited too, very awake now, very alert, her muscles tensing. A sheet and a light blanket confined her; as her intruder began to move again she slid one leg out from under the covers at the side of the bed, and when her foot met the floor she slowly followed it until she was free of the covers and standing.

Her intruder had now arrived at the luggage rack on which rested her suitcase and suddenly a pencil-thin ray of light carved a circle of il-lumination out of the darkness, hung briefly on the wall and then dropped to her open suitcase. As he leaned over it, Mrs. Pollifax moved toward him, thinking this was going to be un-fairly easy if his back remained turned, and no challenge at all. She had just reached him when he stiffened, hearing perhaps the whisper of fabric or catching a movement in the mirror to

his left but it was too late for him: Mrs. Pollifax was already behind him, centering herself,
assuming her stance and turning her hand into
a coiled spring that abruptly shot out now to
hit him at the base of his skull. He gasped,
reeled and started to turn, at which Mrs. Pollifax followed through with a heavier karate slash
to the center of his neck, the first blow con-
fusing him, the second stunning him and sending him unconscious to the floor. Her burglar
had been rendered harmless.

Turning on the light Mrs. Pollifax was astonished to find that it was the Man with the Attaché Case lying at her feet, and this gave her
pause: *not* a hotel thief, she thought, her mind
groping for the implications of this and not
liking them at all when she found them. She
knelt beside the man, felt his pulse, nodded
and went to the phone and dialed Robin's suite.

"Robin, there's a man in my room," she told
him.

He said pleasantly, "For a moment I thought
you said there was a man in your room."

"I did," she told him. "He's here on the floor."

"*Again?*" he said incredulously. "Another?"

"What's more, he's the man who followed me
on Monday afternoon — *he comes from Feng
Imports.*"

There was silence while Robin also groped

toward the implications of this.

"He's unconscious now," she went on, "and I'd guess that he'll remain so for at least an hour, possibly two, but after that—"

"I'll be right down," Robin told her, and hung up.

She was waiting at the door for him when he hurried out of the elevator and down the hall, and she noticed that even at one o'clock in the morning, wearing blue jeans, he looked impossibly handsome and Savile Row.

"Where — ah," he said, entering and seeing the figure sprawled on her rug. "Definitely karate this time."

She nodded. "I woke up and he was — simply there. Or here. And he simply mustn't regain consciousness in my room, Robin."

"Absolutely not," he agreed. "Conversation would be terribly awkward in such circumstances and he could resent very much your having knocked him out."

She ignored this flippancy. "The horror of it — and it's very discouraging to think about," she told him earnestly, "is that whatever we do with him he'll remember that I hit him, and Detwiler will be told, and it will completely destroy my amateur status."

"Completely," he agreed.

"Unless," she added, turning thoughtful,

"unless we could somehow discredit him. After all, he didn't see me, you know...I crept up behind him but he didn't actually *see* me."

Robin's eyes took on a mischievous glint. "Now *that*," he said, "begins to have infinite and wondrous possibilities. He entered a dark room—"

She said excitedly, "Or the *wrong* room?"

"Exactly! In fact if we carry him off to just the right place he could be accused of imagining the whole thing, and no one need believe that he reached you at all! After all, how utterly improbable — how very outrageous! — that Mrs. Pollifax of all people would ever dream of leveling a burglar with a karate chop."

She beamed at him happily, thinking how invigorating it was to work with someone whose mind moved in the same orbit as her own. "Of course we've not even considered why Detwiler sent him here, or for what—"

"Later," he said. "Let us instead get him safely *out*, and bend our thoughts to *where*... *How* is no problem; we carry him between us — to the freight elevator, I suppose, which is becoming habitual — and it will be assumed he's had too much to drink. But where? Let me think..."

Mrs. Pollifax watched him lean against the bureau and think. With a rueful smile he said,

"The Tiger Balm Gardens would be a glorious place to dump him, he'd wake up to all those grotesque figures and have nightmares for weeks, but unfortunately it's closed at this hour. A pity, but I think we must forego such creative possibilities and dump him somewhere in the hotel."

"In the hotel," repeated Mrs. Pollifax, and then, "Prop him up at one of the bars?"

Robin, grinning, said, "On a bar stool, with a Bloody Mary at his elbow?"

"Or there's the basement," she said, "or the kitchens. Or — no, wait," she cried, "I've thought of something. The mall will be empty, won't it?"

"The shops will be dark and closed but it's still an entrance to the hotel, with probably a guard making his stated rounds."

"Perfect," she told him. "Let me get dressed now...trust me!"

When Mrs. Pollifax emerged, fully clothed and in hat, Robin was tucking a wallet back into their burglar's jacket. "He does have a name, it's Allan Chen."

"I rather liked calling him the Man with the Attaché Case," she admitted, "but of course he didn't bring his attaché case tonight. Shall we take Mr. Chen away now?"

Slowly they staggered down the hall with

Mr. Chen sagging between them, and were fortunate in meeting no one in the hall. The freight elevator descended and Mrs. Pollifax, recalling her numerous passages and exits through the mall, hoped that her memory was accurate. The doors slid open and Mrs. Pollifax peered out, uncertain just where the elevator had delivered them and explaining to Robin, "It's between the shop selling magazines and the shop selling Chinese Buddhas."

"What is?" asked Robin, leaning hard against Mr. Chen to hold him pinned to the wall. "Is the mall empty? He's getting damned heavy."

"I'll reconnoiter," she said, and left him to peer around the corner. Returning, she signaled to him. "It's just to the right, and only a few paces, but do let's hurry!"

"Nothing would delight me more," said Robin, peeling Mr. Chen from the wall and receiving him into his arms. "What are we heading *toward?*"

"A machine...good heavens," she gasped, "he *has* grown heavy hasn't he, but — there it is."

Robin stared in astonishment. "But what on earth is it?"

"You haven't seen one before? It measures blood pressure — at home they seem to have them everywhere now, in movie houses, supermarkets, the oddest places...You sit on that bench and place that strap around your wrist and then you drop money into the slot and your blood pressure lights up on the screen just like a pinball machine."

"How very amazing," Robin said, staring at it, "and how much more creative than a mere bar stool." He gently lowered Mr. Chen to the bench and Mrs. Pollifax wrapped and secured the strap around his wrist; tenderly they lowered Mr. Chen's head to the shelf to forestall his falling across it, and then, consulting the machine's directions, and before she could stop him, Robin dropped four Hong Kong coins into the slot.

"Robin!" she protested.

"Blood pressure a bit high," he murmured, standing back to observe the flashing numbers.

"I doubt that mine's exactly normal at this moment either," she said crossly. "I'm hearing footsteps, Robin — hurry!"

"Yes," said Robin, retreating with her to the corner from which they'd emerged, "but Mr. Chen is safely removed from your room at last, and just look at our handiwork."

Mrs. Pollifax turned and looked, and her last glimpse of Mr. Chen was of him slumped over the console, as if studiously and nearsightedly studying its directions, while the screen above

him continued to flash 150/72...150/72...
150/72 in bright red lights.

"For myself," said Robin, ushering her into
the elevator, "this has been a very educational
interlude, which I think calls for a steadying
drink. Have they replaced your brandy?"

"They replace everything, making little notes
in their notebooks," she told him.

"Good, because I think you could use one,
too. I realize that you're accustomed to men
stumbling into your room at all hours of the
night but you surely must be feeling the strain."

"Actually," she confessed, "I feel more like
laughing."

Robin nodded. "Definitely hysteria looms."
When they arrived at the sixth floor, he led
her back to her room and poured them each a
brandy. "All right, let's do a quick probe here,
bearing in mind that we meet for breakfast in
only a few hours. Just what do you think has
drawn Detwiler's attention to you?"

She shook her head. "I'd know better if I
could think what Mr. Chen was looking for in
my room. I'm sure that I wasn't followed today, and I'd swear that Detwiler had by now
concluded that I'm harmless. The only possibility I can think of is that Detwiler phoned
Mrs. O'Malley tonight and she described my
visit and my appearance to him."

"How possible is that on a scale of one to ten?"

"A scant one," she told him. "Mrs. O'Malley hasn't heard from him in two months."

"Then what's in your suitcase that he was about to search? Or your purse, for instance, or—"

He stopped and he and Mrs. Pollifax stared at each other. "The gun — the Beretta," she said. "I'd forgotten about it, do you think he was after the gun?"

Robin frowned, looking puzzled. "The gun would certainly tie Detwiler to Inspector Hao's murder all right. That would mean someone had to be watching our arrival at the hut this morning — or yesterday morning — which wouldn't surprise me, in which case they'd know that one of us walked off with the murder weapon."

"But why me? Why would they think I'd have the gun?" protested Mrs. Pollifax. "It could have been you or Mr. Hitchens just as easily, and they simply *couldn't* have seen me pocket it. And why would they want the Beretta back *now*, when the only fingerprints on it are mine? It doesn't feel right, Robin."

"Nor to me either," he said, "but you'd better get rid of the blasted thing soon, anyway." He sighed. "I think some sleep is in order, don't you? Court tells me that one of the integral sayings of Zen Buddhism is, 'Do the best you can and then walk on.' Well, we've done the best we can tonight, so let's walk on. Think you can sleep?"

She aborted a yawn and smiled at him. "You must tell me more sometime soon about Court's interest in Zen...Yes, I can sleep — after I've propped a chair against my door, dragged the night table in front of it, and laid a few other ambushes."

He nodded and absently kissed the top of her head as he passed. "I'll let you get on with it, then. See you at eight!"

He made his exit, leaving Mrs. Pollifax not only to rearrange furniture but to ponder again what she might have done to lift Mr. Detwiler's suspicions of her.

# 10

When Mrs. Pollifax arrived at Robin's suite
the next morning at eight, Mr. Hitchens was
already there. "Sssh," counseled Robin, opening the door to her and pointing to Mr. Hitchens, who sat upright on the couch with his
eyes closed.

Mrs. Pollifax tiptoed in and sat down, seeing
that in one hand Mr. Hitchens held the fragment of newspaper bearing Eric the Red's
photo.

He said now, his eyes remaining closed,
"You gave me this slip of paper without showing it to me, and the impression I get very
strongly is that it's the picture of a man, and —
it's really strange — I feel that I've seen this
man before. This piece of paper has been
handled frequently by someone who wrote a
word on it somewhere, in a very heavy scrawl,
and I can only tell you that the word was writ-

ten in a mood of anger and frustration." He opened his eyes. "You hoped I might come up with a date – I'm sorry." He saw Mrs. Pollifax and smiled. "Good morning!"

"Good morning," she said cheerfully.

"You can look at it now," Robin told him. "The word written there is WHEN, as you can see. You've absolutely no answer to that scribbled 'when'?"

Mr. Hitchens shook his head. "No, because whoever wrote it didn't know the answer, and I can only pick up what he or she knew at the time." Glancing down at the picture he said in astonishment, "But this is the man we saw on the plane!" He looked at Mrs. Pollifax. "You remember? You pointed him out to me, you'd stepped on his foot!"

Mrs. Pollifax beamed at him happily. "So you recognize him, too. We found it yesterday in Inspector Hao's house – which quite frankly we burgled after leaving you – and it's he who scrawled the 'when' across the photo...Alec's father."

"Good heavens!" said Mr. Hitchens.

Robin nodded. "Yes, and having jeopardized my job by insisting on three men being flown in last night, all on the strength of Mrs. Pollifax recognizing him, I can't tell you how relieved I am to hear you confirm its being the same man."

"But — who is he?" asked Mr. Hitchens, puzzled. "And you've not found Alec, what *have* you discovered? And three men being flown in for *what?*"

Robin turned to Mrs. Pollifax. "Care to take this on? I'd like to hear it said out loud to see if I've gone mad or am only too sane."

Mrs. Pollifax nodded. "It's grown much bigger than a missing man and a murder, Mr. Hitchens; we think we know what Alec's father discovered that led to his being kidnapped and then murdered. The man you and I saw on the plane is the same terrorist who directed the Cairo assassination and the French hostage affair, and now he's in Hong Kong."

Mr. Hitchens looked appalled. "But he's the man no one can find...he's — wait a minute, Eric the Red they call him, the Liberation 80's leader?"

Mrs. Pollifax nodded. "Yes, and on Monday morning, after we'd breakfasted together, you and I, I saw him coming out of Feng Imports, an obscure little shop in an obscure alley where I happened to be looking for a young man I met in China last year. Then, as you know, I met Robin, who happens to have come to Hong Kong because of mysterious rumors about this area, and by accident—"

Mr. Hitchens shook his head. "Nothing happens by accident," he said firmly. "Nothing."

Somewhat taken aback, Robin said, "Be that as it may, Mrs. Pollifax and I met and it looks now as if our two missions are amalgamating, so to speak. We've put a watch on Feng Imports, hoping Eric the Red may return there, but whether he does or not, he's here in Hong Kong, and although it's possible that he may have come to visit an ailing Aunt Hortense it's extremely unlikely under the circumstances. Putting all the facts together it would seem that something — *something* — is due to happen here."

Mr. Hitchens whistled. "Except you don't know what."

"Or when," said Robin. "Or how, or where... Mr. Hitchens, can you help us?"

He said fervently, "I'll do everything possible — I will, I will, and I can assure you—" A knock at the door interrupted him.

"That will be our breakfast, I ordered it for eight o'clock on the button." Robin glanced at his watch as he strode toward the door. "While the waiter brings it in I suggest we turn on the news and hear if there've been any developments on Hao's murder — but softly, because Marko's sleeping — and postpone serious business until we've eaten."

The police, according to the newscast, were still looking for Alec Hao and distributing flyers with his photograph – it was shown on the screen – and searching for the murder weapon, at which point the glances of both Robin and Mr. Hitchens flew to Mrs. Pollifax's purse on the couch, and she made a face and nodded. There was no further news; police were still pursuing a number of leads, and to wrap it up Mr. Hitchens appeared again on the screen in a replay of his earlier interview.

"Well done!" said Robin, snapping off the set. "Now I refuse all shop talk, my digestion demands it, we speak of cabbages and kings, please, and myriad other things."

Mrs. Pollifax smiled. "All right – Cyrus is coming," she announced. "There was a cable last night; he expects to be here by tomorrow evening."

"Marvelous," said Robin, beaming at her. "I shall be able to give Court a full report on him. And how was your night on the town, Mr. Hitchens?"

Mr. Hitchens said almost shyly, "That was wonderful, too. Ruthie and I did a little dancing but mostly we talked and talked and talked. Her tour's here until Saturday." He turned to Mrs. Pollifax. "We're meeting later this morning for a short cruise of the harbor. Would you care to come with us? Ruthie would like to meet you again, she said so."

Mrs. Pollifax, interrupting a breakfast of ham and eggs, bean curd, papaya, watermelon, bacon, sausage and orange juice, toast and coffee, said that she would be delighted to accompany them.

"High time Mrs. P. did some sightseeing," contributed Robin. "All work and no play, and all that. Tell us about Ruthie, Mr. Hitchens, the wife who didn't mind your being quiet and dull, as you phrased it."

Slowly, awkwardly, Mr. Hitchens began to speak of Ruthie, and Mrs. Pollifax discovered that her guesses had been surprisingly accurate: they'd been high school sweethearts and had married young, after which she'd been the only woman he'd looked at for ten years.

"But then — I *don't* know how it was," Mr. Hitchens said fiercely, with a scowl as he glared into his past.

They waited to hear how it was, Robin's fork suspended in midair and Mrs. Pollifax studying Mr. Hitchens's scowl while she sipped her coffee.

"I guess what happened," said Mr. Hitchens unhappily, "was that my first book on psychic phenomena was published, I was interviewed on a Boston talk-show and met Sophie Simms."

"Ah," murmured Robin and his fork went into motion again.

"Sophie was an actress?" prompted Mrs. Pollifax.

Mr. Hitchens nodded, looking acutely miserable. "Trying to be, yes — with the longest eyelashes I'd ever seen...She'd been doing improvisations in a small nightclub, and I think I've already told you that being psychic is of *no* help where my own life is involved."

Robin asked gently, "And how long did it last?"

"It was horrible for Ruthie — horrible," went on Mr. Hitchens, his eyes fixed blindly on his plate of food, "and I can't tell you how it surprises me that she even agreed to spend an evening with me. I was completely dazzled — hypnotized, really, I suppose. Sophie was so — so — well, it was all so *glamorous.*" His glance lifted from his plate to advance to the pink rose at the center of the table. "I felt — it's hard to explain, but I felt so initiated into such a feminine world." He shook his head. "Just watching Sophie put on her makeup every morning, for instance, was — well, like watching Cezanne mix colors on his palette, it was so intimate, such a ritual...And her clothes — I helped her look for just the right sort, they had to be rather outrageous, you know, and—" He broke off and

168

sighed. "To answer your question, there was one good year, but only because I was so dazzled, and then two more years before she wandered off with a third-rate producer who she hoped would be of more use to her career than I had been." He added sadly, "He wasn't."

"No, they never are," said Robin. "I believe you mentioned a third − er −"

"Mistake? Misadventure?" Mr. Hitchens's laugh was bitter. "Oh yes, Sophie had a friend... that was Rosalie, also in show business. I'd given Rosalie readings − without charge, of course − and she was very sympathetic over everything that happened with Sophie, and listened to all my problems, and of course didn't realize that being married to a psychic wouldn't advance *her* career, either." He shook his head. "I have been − I scarcely need say − very naïve as well as very immature."

"Yes," said Mrs. Pollifax calmly.

He gave her a reproachful glance. "You don't have to agree so flatly; no one enjoys hearing the truth."

Robin said lightly, "I had no idea the life of a professional psychic could be so hazardous but I can agree with you on glamour becoming addictive. It certainly seduced me for a long time and I went to great lengths to enter the world of Beautiful People − however illicitly," he added with a humorous glance at Mrs. Pollifax. "After all, I started out in life as the son of a London locksmith, dropping all my *h*'s, and ended up hobnobbing with sheiks and princes."

Mr. Hitchens looked at him in surprise. "You did?"

"But none of them had long eyelashes," Robin said gravely.

Mr. Hitchens shook his head. "I appreciate your sympathy but I feel — have felt since that third divorce over a year ago — so ashamed, really. You see, I always wanted — always planned — to live a life of the spirit — I hope that doesn't sound pretentious? — and all I've learned is how weak and shallow a person I am."

"Nonsense," said Mrs. Pollifax sturdily, "we all betray ourselves from time to time or how else would we find out what our selves are? I refuse your hair shirt, Mr. Hitchens, you're missing the point...namely it's where you are *now* that matters."

His scowl had returned. "What do you mean?"

"Well, feel ashamed if you must," she told him, "but look at Robin if you will. He lifted himself out of a frustrating environment into one where he could use his considerable talents and craft — however illicitly," she added with a mischievous glance at Robin, "but if he hadn't done this – in the only way he saw how, at the time – he would never have acquired the specialized skills or been in a position to join and appreciate Interpol, where presumably he's of great help in policing the world–"

"Hear! hear!" murmured Robin.

"–and he'd certainly never have met his wife Court, whom he loves dearly. Whereas you, Mr. Hitchens – you wouldn't be here in Hong Kong this morning, attempting to solve a murder, making headline news in the paper and meeting Ruthie again – if two women hadn't spun you dizzily off balance and left you open to coming here, now would you? If living is a process, then how does one arrive anywhere except by just such painful routes?"

Mr. Hitchens looked at her with interest. "You too?"

Mrs. Pollifax laughed. "Of course! It wasn't *that* long ago that I felt my life totally useless and wondered if it was worth continuing. Actually a doctor found me depressed enough to urge that I look for some work I'd always wanted to do – and off I went to apply for work as a spy! Which I must say changed my life considerably," she added humorously, "but this is *not* finding Alec, is it, or using Mr. Hitchens's considerable talent."

171

"Amazing," Mr. Hitchens said, staring at her.

"Of course," Robin told him with a quick, warm smile.

"Last night I felt quite strongly that Alec's still alive," Mr. Hitchens said shyly. He turned his attention away from Mrs. Pollifax but occasionally he glanced back at her with frank curiosity.

Robin said, "Is there some way you could find out — psychically — if it's Hong Kong itself, rather than Kowloon or New Territories or Macao, where Eric the Red plans his drama?"

"Drama!" said Mr. Hitchens.

Robin shrugged. "That's what terrorism is, basically — pure theater. Nothing in particular is ever accomplished by it, other than to focus attention on a small group of people who seize absolute power by threatening everything that holds civilization together."

"Absolute power," mused Mrs. Pollifax. "Like monstrous children thumbing their noses at adults who live by codes and laws and scruples."

Robin said in a hard voice, "In my line of work I've tangled with narcotic dealers and suppliers — that's Interpol's job — and I can say of them that at least they give value for their money. If what they sell destroys human lives their victims cooperate by choice in their own destruction, and if drug dealers bend and

172

break every law in the book they at least *know* the laws.

"But terrorists—" He shook his head. "They're the parasites of the century. They want to make a statement, they simply toss a bomb or round up innocent people to hold hostage, or kill without compunction, remorse or compassion. If they need money, they simply rob a bank. I have to admit not only my contempt for them," he added, "but my fear, too, because their only passion is to mock and to destroy, and that really *is* frightening."

"Antilife," murmured Mrs. Pollifax, remembering Eric the Red's glance on the plane.

Mr. Hitchens said abruptly, "Get me a map — as many maps as you have."

Robin brought him maps: street maps of Hong Kong, of Kowloon, of New Territories and of Macao. Mr. Hitchens laid them out flat, side by side, on the long table and asked for silence.

"You've got it," said Robin.

Mr. Hitchens closed his eyes and sat quietly for a long time, until the ticking of a nearby clock seemed to fill the room. At last he lifted one hand and began slowly moving it across the surface of the maps, sometimes in a circular motion, sometimes up and down, several times lingering briefly in one place. Five minutes passed and then abruptly he dropped his hand to one of the maps and opened his eyes. "This area," he said, and removing a pen from his pocket he drew a circle. "This brings very uncomfortable feelings, a sense of violence, and very disturbing vibrations."

"Central Hong Kong," murmured Mrs. Pollifax, leaning closer to look. "Downtown Hong Kong?"

"Your circle takes in a large area," Robin said in a troubled voice, "and it doesn't even include Feng Imports."

Mr. Hitchens shrugged. "Perhaps to both, but there are guns somewhere inside this circle, and one that looks like this. Paper, someone?"

Mrs. Pollifax handed him a paper napkin and watched his nimble fingers block out lines. "Like this," he said.

Robin, staring at his sketch, said in horror, "But you've just drawn the outline of a multiple rocket launcher!"

"Have I?" said Mr. Hitchens indifferently. "I don't know what it is, I've only sketched what I saw."

Robin sat back and frankly gaped — his mouth was actually open in shock — and Mrs. Pollifax wondered if he had really grasped Mr. Hitchens's possibilities before this moment. She said softly, "Intelligence groups *are* using psychics,

174

you know...I've read of it even in newspapers. The CIA...the Soviets..."

"But — but Mr. Hitchens has never *seen* a rocket launcher," protested Robin. "And yet he's drawn one. I mean, it's uncanny."

"Of course," said Mrs. Pollifax, amused, for having had her life saved in Turkey by just such means she was herself beyond astonishment.

"Then they have to have a radio," Robin said, suddenly closing his mouth and rallying. "The circle doesn't include Feng Imports and if that circle is accurate, and if eleven members of the Liberation 80's are hiding inside that circle, and Detwiler is the mastermind of this project, there would have to be communication and my guess would be a high-powered radio." He nodded. "I think it's time I visit the Governor, I think it's time we risk some of Hong Kong's police being brought into this because it's time we have radio-detection vans cruising the streets checking for high-power transmissions. We're going to need help, it's too big a responsibility for a handful of people." He reached for the napkin with a wry smile. "I hope you don't mind if I take this along with me as evidence? I don't know quite how His Excellency will react to — to—"

Mr. Hitchens smiled forgivingly. "By all

means take it."

Robin had just pocketed the napkin when the telephone rang; he moved swiftly to the desk and snatched it up on the first ring. "Yes?"

He listened, made a note on the pad in front of him and said, "Thanks enormously." Hanging up he turned to Mrs. Pollifax. "That Donald Chang to whom Sheng Ti delivered a packet of diamonds...I phoned my superiors in Paris last night, thinking it wiser *they* call the Hong Kong police officially with an inquiry about the chap. That was Paris calling: Donald Chang works in the baggage room at Kai Tak airport."

"Aha," said Mrs. Pollifax.

Robin, shrugging into a flawlessly cut black linen jacket, nodded. "Exactly. I can't think of a better place for anyone engaged in the smuggling racket, for which the payoff could be one packet of diamonds from Detwiler at Feng Imports — another little tidbit for His Excellency." He saluted each of them with a smile. "I'm off...I wish you a delightful cruise in Hong Kong harbor — see you later!"

# 11

The harbor and the sky were sunless this morning and a gauze curtain of mist had swept over
the mountains to soften and blur their shapes
and obscure their peaks. A cold choppy wind
blew across the water, and once aboard the
launch Mrs. Pollifax shivered; a light had been
turned off and without its radiance the brilliant
tropical greens looked sullen; earth-browns that
had been invisible until now outweighed the
greens in prominence, bringing a somber dull-
ness to the landscape that was relieved only by
the orange of a tile roof on the wooded hill-
sides or the snowy façade of a new block of
high-rise buildings. A jolly Raoul Dufy had
become a moody Turner.

   Mrs. Pollifax had joined Ruthie and Mr.
Hitchens not merely to sightsee for two hours;
she had the more practical purpose of gun-
disposal, and being in possession of a murder

weapon, she considered the harbor an excellent place in which to bury it forever. She felt no compunction about her illegal act, because at the moment she could think of no explanation for having the gun that would appease the police. But she admitted also to an interest in seeing Ruthie and Mr. Hitchens together; anything so unusual as two people accidentally meeting again thousands of miles from home tugged at her curiosity. The odds against it, she felt, were surely five million to one, and the coincidences of timing — of their being in Hong Kong on the same day, and of their arriving in the lobby of the same hotel at the same moment — thoroughly charmed her.

It had obviously charmed Ruthie, too, for she looked younger today and it was not entirely due to her wearing red slacks and a bright red shirt and kerchief; she looked transformed, as almost all women do when feeling courted. She called Mr. Hitchens "Hitch," to which Mrs. Pollifax reacted with amusement and a faint sense of shock, for she herself couldn't imagine calling him anything but Mr. Hitchens. She tried to picture what he might have been like when the two had met in high school, and she smiled as she set to work stripping him of his pedantic quality, enlarging on the boyishly delighted Mr. Hitchens who had crept out of the hotel by the rear entrance, adding a touch more shyness and removing five pounds and the hint of gray at his temples.

"What are you smiling at?" asked Ruthie, shouting above the wind and the sound of the engines.

They had taken places in the stern, away from the spray as the launch headed out into the harbor to thread its way among trawlers, sampans, pleasure boats, cargo ships and junks, but before Mrs. Pollifax could reply Mr. Hitchens shouted, "Coffee? They've opened up the snack counter!"

"Oh *yes,*" said Mrs. Pollifax with feeling, and as he moved across the desk, staggering a little against the wind, she said, "I was just wondering what he was like when you met in high school."

Ruthie laughed. "Oh — very serious and very bookish, and feeling that being psychic couldn't possibly equal playing on the football team."

"And you loved him."

Ruthie gave her a quick, startled glance and looked just as quickly away. "Yes." She hesitated, looking embarrassed, and then she said with a controlled lightness. "Do you think that — well, old fires can be rekindled?"

Mrs. Pollifax smiled. "I don't see why on earth they should be," she said. "I think it far more interesting — and a great deal more fun — to simply begin all fresh and new."

Ruthie looked startled. "You mean — not try again but look for someone else fresh and new."

Mrs. Pollifax touched her hand. "Not at all, and if we're talking about you and Mr. Hitchens — and I can't think who else we'd be speaking of — I mean that whatever drew you together once can certainly draw you together again now but I think it a great mistake to look at it as a continuation. After all, you're different people now."

Ruthie said ruefully, "What drew him to me, according to my therapist, was his looking for a mother. Except that he outgrew that and wanted to enjoy his lost youth with Sophie and then Rosalie."

Mrs. Pollifax laughed. "What a pat explanation! Well, I rather think he encountered too *much* youth, from hearing him speak of it, and he just may have grown bored with motherhood after having to mother *them*. The young so frequently have no conversation, I find, and for myself I cannot imagine anything more frustrating than living with someone who didn't experience the horrors of the Kennedy assassination, or even know who Clark Gable was."

Ruthie laughed. "That's refreshing, you almost make my doubts disappear."

Mrs. Pollifax looked at her with a twinkle in her eye. "Doubts — or fears? You know," she said, reaching over and clasping her hand for a moment, "I really think he's seeing you with fresh eyes — he seems so astonished by it all — which leaves it entirely up to you. Did you make a very *good* new life? Oh thank you," she said to Mr. Hitchens, who returned with three coffees in Styrofoam cups.

Ruthie said with pride, "Yes I did, I moved into a charming apartment in Boston, in a very old house; I began teaching a fifth grade instead of kindergarten, and I started traveling."

"And has she traveled!" exclaimed Mr. Hitchens, leaning forward to join their conversation. "She leaves Saturday for Bangkok, can you imagine?"

Mrs. Pollifax sipped her coffee and listened to them talk of travel, and then of Boston, and she decided that all was well between Ruthie and Mr. Hitchens. When the proper moment arrived she made her way to the railing, opened her purse and casually dropped overboard the gun that had killed Inspector Hao. With that done, she settled down to the remaining hour of their cruise, to glimpses of white beaches at Repulse Bay and the city of sampans at Aberdeen, but her thoughts began to wander back to Feng Imports and to Mr. Detwiler, and she began to consider both of them from a new angle that startled her because over and over the question persisted: *why hadn't Detwiler visited his home for two months?*

"Why Irma Blank!" exclaimed Mrs. O'Malley, a huge smile enveloping her face. "To think you've come back! How nice."

"Hello," said Mrs. Pollifax, smiling. "I found myself on the next street and thought I'd just stop in and say hello and—"

"And just in time for a spot of tea," said Mrs. O'Malley in her rich, authoritative voice. "Come in, come in, I was about to pour meself a cup. Feet tired, dear?"

Deceit, thought Mrs. Pollifax, was really difficult with this kindly woman; after all, she'd had an excellent lunch of soup, steamed dumplings, bean curd and for dessert two coconut snowballs, and except for a stroll back to the hotel to change into survey clothes she had been sitting for most of the day. "Terribly," she said with a sigh, "I'll really have to think about that housekeeping you suggested, although I did very well today with my surveys." She followed Mrs. O'Malley into the kitchen and as she sat down she placed her newspaper on the table, carefully arranged so that Alec Hao's photograph was prominent.

"Oh, that dear boy," said Mrs. O'Malley, catching sight of the newspaper as she poured tea. "The only son, too!"

"Oh?" said Mrs. Pollifax. "Did you ever—" She paused, wanting to approach the matter obliquely but to settle once and for all if Alec had passed through this house after being kidnapped. "Have your paths ever crossed?" she asked.

Mrs. O'Malley, seating herself across the table, said, "Oh no, dear, for he's been in college in the United States, you know, doing very well, even graduating with Latin words after his name."

Mrs. Pollifax stared at her in astonishment. "How — that is — I don't recall reading that in the paper."

"No, no," Mrs. O'Malley told her soothingly, "it's from his father I heard it, may God rest his soul. Really proud of him, his father was."

"His father," echoed Mrs. Pollifax. "You knew his father. The man found dead yesterday."

She nodded. "Oh, many's the night he's been here for dinner, he and Mr. Detwiler being friends, yes. Such a nice man he was, too, the inspector, and how he loved my Beggar's Chicken! It's baked eight hours in a clay pot, you know—"

Mrs. Pollifax sat stunned: Mr. Detwiler and Inspector Hao friends? The two men had not only known each other but were *friends?* She felt herself reeling as she sat and allowed Mrs. O'Malley's words to flow over her.

"—chicken stuffed with chestnuts, herbs and shredded cabbage and then wrapped in lotus leaves..."

Mrs. Pollifax wet her lips, which felt suddenly dry, and said mechanically, "It sounds delicious."

"Oh, very special it is, yes," agreed Mrs. O'Malley.

"You could open a restaurant then," Mrs. Pollifax suggested. "That is, if ever you tire of keeping house for Mr. Detwiler." The circle was growing smaller, she thought, struggling to remain steady in the face of Mrs. O'Malley's casually imparted news. Two men in this strange confusion of clues had been in contact. Two points were converging: they had been friends, and at this Mrs. Pollifax began to feel a sense of excitement... Had the Inspector confided to his friend his growing suspicions of briberies and stolen passports, never realizing that Detwiler was heavily involved in both, and that it would lead to the Inspector's death? Or could it have been Detwiler who inadvertently dropped the clue for Inspector Hao that had begun the search that killed him?

Well, at least she had established once and for all — and this had troubled her — that Alec Hao had never passed through Detwiler's house after being kidnapped, but she admitted that she was appalled by the fact that they had been good friends, Detwiler and the dead Inspector.

"And Mr. Feng, did he come to dinner here, too?" she asked.

Mrs. O'Malley shook her head. "Oh no, *he* was never invited." From her dismissing tone Mrs. Pollifax deduced that he was not considered dinner-party material.

They continued their gossip for another half an hour. Mrs. Pollifax struggled earnestly to maintain her role of Irma Blank, but it was difficult, and when she at last excused herself she felt drained. At the door she said, "I'll not be in the same neighborhood tomorrow but it's been a real pleasure, Mrs. O'Malley. No news yet, I suppose, of your employer's return?"

Mrs. O'Malley's eyes brightened. "Now would you believe it, he sent word by the delivery boy this morning — the lad what brings his laundry — that it's the last he'll be needing done, as he hopes to be comin' home late next week."

"Late next week," repeated Mrs. Pollifax, blinking at this second staggering piece of news. "Oh, how very nice..." and thanking her again for tea, Mrs. Pollifax walked to the street feeling that she had come here to fish for a minnow and had instead pulled in two whales.

Mrs. Pollifax found Marko alone in the suite when she reached it, and when she had told him her news he nodded thoughtfully. "So..." he mused, "so it is possible that late next week it will all be over and Robin's instincts were right, we have arrived for the conclusion, not the beginning of it." He shook his head. "We now – how do you call it – batten down the hatches?"

"Yes, and where is Robin?"

"Of that I have not the foggiest," Marko said, with a glance at his watch. "It is already past four...He spent the morning with the Governor, and he's no doubt meeting now with the head of Hong Kong's special police unit, to brief him and to arrange for a radio-detection van—"

"Tell me about those vans," said Mrs. Pollifax.

Marko perched on the edge of the couch. "Gladly, but I will have to make it brief because I have the four-thirty-to-midnight shift at Dragon Alley, and for telling Robin of your grave discoveries you must leave a note to him. For the van there is a driver and the truck is a closed unit, bristling with aerials inside that are operated by two men who turn the aerials with great care, ready to pick up any activity. Once there is action they plot the course of the coded signals they are picking up, turning those aerials until they cross and pinpoint the location of secret radio transmitters."

"I see. And then they have found the hiding place!"

Marko smiled wryly. "Only sometimes, and only if they are very very quick about it, because anyone sending code signals transmits for a very short time — two and a half minutes and they are beyond the safe limit."

"That's not very helpful, is it," she said indignantly.

Marko laughed and reached over to pinch her cheek affectionately. "No of course not, but why should they be helpful? After two and a half minutes they are vulnerable to anyone who might wish to find them, who might even — consider! — send out radio-detection vans to comb the streets and listen. In this game nothing is easy, and one mistake—" He lifted a hand and ran a finger from left to right across his throat. *Finis.*"

"Yes," said Mrs. Pollifax, watching him lift his jacket and slip a gun into his holster. "Any news from the men watching Feng Imports?"

"Nothing. I do not myself think we will see Eric the Red there again, and where he is hiding I would give my right arm to know."

"Surely not your right arm," she protested. "Isn't that rather exorbitant?"

"You think so? I will tell you," he said, pausing in his preparations. "I will tell you of my cousin Gena Constantine who was eighteen years old three years ago, very eager, very fresh and lovely, with a cockeyed sense of humor. You understand not all women in my family are lovely – some are fat, some have moustaches, but Gena was special." Without expression he added, "And then one day she walked into a bank in Paris and a bomb goes off, and after that there is not much remaining of my cousin Gena, not even to bury."

"Oh, Marko," she breathed.

"So I do not like terrorists," he said simply, and picking up a book – Mrs. Pollifax saw that it was Lecomte du Noüy's *Human Destiny* – he placed it in his knapsack and said, "Now I am ready. And you – you are maybe a little excited about your Cyrus on his way?"

She nodded.

"Enjoy!" And blowing her a kiss he went out, leaving Mrs. Pollifax to contemplate dinner and a welcome early bedtime once she had written her note to Robin describing her discoveries of the afternoon.

But her day had not ended once she settled herself in bed that evening, for she had finally gained the time and leisure to consider the happenings of the past three days and to try and place pieces of the puzzle in juxtaposition. There were, for instance, a number of discrepancies that clamored for explanation, not to mention pieces that refused to fit as they should.

Should. Ought. Scenarios again, she thought crossly, which was how the mind persistently worked, using facts and assumptions left over from the past to draw conclusions that were frequently in error.

What was needed, she decided firmly, was to empty her mind of facts and to begin freshly, with nothing at all preconceived.

She did not immediately push it, however; she began instead to think of all that had taken place since she had arrived in Hong Kong... of her visit to Feng Imports, of Detwiler — charming and unctuous in his black silk suit with the gold cuff links — and his gift to her of a Buddha... of Mr. Feng, who looked like an ivory figurine himself... of Sheng Ti and Lotus and of the missing Alec Hao, of Mrs. O'Malley, and of her own whispered promise to the dead Inspector as she'd left the hut...

and then she erased all impressions from her mind and waited.

When — sometime later — she opened her eyes it was to whisper, "But of course, how *blind* of me!"

She understood now why Detwiler hadn't visited his home for two months, and she guessed why he had given her the Buddha. Picking up the phone, she dictated a cable to Carstairs in Baltimore. When she had completed this she turned off the light, and before she could even wonder how soon her suppositions might be tested she slipped into a tranquil sleep.

# 12

# THURSDAY

Mrs. Pollifax awoke the next morning to the sound of a buzz ringing urgently in her ears and summoning her attention. She opened one eye experimentally, saw that day had arrived, opened the other eye and established from a glance at her clock that it was nine, and that it was not her alarm clock ringing. Reaching for the phone she was happy to discover that once she lifted the receiver the noise stopped. "Hello," she said sleepily.

"This is Mrs. Pollifax speaking?" inquired a suave male voice.

Mrs. Pollifax at once sat up, suddenly alert, and assured the voice that yes, she was Mrs. Pollifax.

"This is Mr. Detwiler from the Feng Import

Company, whom you may remember meeting several days ago?"

She did not mention that she had immediately recognized his voice. "Yes indeed," she said warmly, "and I have certainly been enjoying the Buddha you were so kind as to give me."

There was the briefest of silences and then he said, "Which makes it so difficult, what I must say, Mrs. Pollifax, for it is about the Buddha I am calling."

Concealing her interest, Mrs. Pollifax said merely, "Oh?" while her eyes moved to the serenely glowing Buddha across the room.

"Yes, for it seems that I did Mr. Feng a *great* disservice when I chose that particular one for you, Mrs. Pollifax, it is a Buddha that was carved specially for a monastery in Kyota, Japan. It has taken some time to discover that it is this one I gave to you, and it is most embarrassing for me — I cannot tell you how embarrassing — but I must ask if you will return it to me. I will, of course, present you with another, this goes without saying, as well as with my deepest apologies."

"How very unfortunate," she murmured, as her mind raced over the implications of this and she began to feel very pleased.

"Yes it is. We have many Buddhas, as you know, and — I cannot tell you how sorry but I must ask if it can be returned to me here this morning so that it may be wrapped and shipped by afternoon. You could do this?"

There was an appeal in his voice of which Mrs. Pollifax was not unaware, but in any case she had already reached her decision. "Yes I can," she told him cordially, "but I must tell you that I've only just waked up and am neither dressed nor breakfasted, so that I couldn't possibly return it before eleven."

"Apology must be heaped upon apology," he said, but there was a difference in his voice now, a relievedness. "If I may expect you then at eleven?"

"At eleven, yes," she told him gravely, and hung up and sat still for several minutes, going over his words and nodding as she saw pieces of the puzzle slip into place. She did not question why Mr. Detwiler had made no offer to retrieve the Buddha personally; she had not expected it of him.

Dialing Robin's suite she was relieved when he answered promptly. "Things are starting to happen," she told him. "I've just had a telephone call from Mr. Detwiler. Can you and Marko come to my room?"

"A call from Detwiler!" exclaimed Marko. "Be there at once."

"No, slowly — I need five minutes to dress,"

she told him, and hung up. But she did not immediately dress: she dialed room service, ordered breakfast for one and coffee for three before she exchanged pajamas for a jumper and blouse.

"What did he say?" demanded Robin when she opened the door to him and Marko.

"Softly, my friend," said Marko, following him into the room. "Good morning, Mrs. P.!"

"Good morning," she said cheerfully. "Please sit down, both of you, because I've rather much to say to you. My breakfast's on the way, and coffee for you, and I need both your help and your witnessing of something I must do before going to visit Feng Imports this morning at Mr. Detwiler's invitation."

"*What?*" thundered Robin. "Of course you're not going to visit Feng Imports, are you out of your mind?"

Marko, watching her, said, "Hear her out, my friend. One may ask why he makes this invitation to you?"

"Of course. It seems there has been a — a slight error with the Buddhas," she said without expression, "and the one he gave me was designed especially for a monastery in Kyoto."

"For heaven's sake you don't believe him, do you?" said Robin.

Marko, his eyes still on her face, said softly,

"No, she doesn't believe him, Robin. You are volatile this morning, stop pacing and sit!"

Mrs. Pollifax responded to a knock on her door and the waiter wheeled in her breakfast, bowed and went out. Pouring coffee, she handed each a cup, looked without interest at her egg, took a bite and poured herself a cup of coffee. "I told you I had much to say, and it will be in some detail, because the details are important to what I came to understand last night."

"We give you attention," said Marko, looking amused.

"I've come to the conclusion," she told them, "that Carstairs has been all wrong about Mr. Detwiler, and therefore I've been all wrong about him, too."

"And what makes you think that?" asked Robin suspiciously.

"Detail one," she said, holding up a finger. "On my visit to Feng Imports on Monday it occurred to me at the time to wonder why Detwiler invited me into his workshop when Mr. Feng had already told me that he'd never heard of Sheng Ti. Mr. Detwiler was insistent that I join him in the rear, and there was a very sharp exchange with Mr. Feng about this, who was forced to swallow his anger. And two," she added, holding up a second finger, "he insisted on giving me a very exquisite Buddha."

Their eyes moved to the Buddha standing on the bureau. "A remarkably lovely one, yes," said Marko, nodding.

"But a Buddha he now wants back," pointed out Robin dryly.

"Yes, isn't that odd?" she said lightly. "Detail three," she continued. "He also asked to see the slip of paper on which Bishop had scribbled the address of Feng Imports, and looking at it he said — which for the moment I missed — 'You could have received this from only one source, no one else could possibly know of Sheng Ti's presence here.'"

"So why not?" asked Robin. "He's worked for Carstairs for years, hasn't he? He could very well have recognized Bishop's handwriting."

"Yes, I agree with you," she said. "He *did* recognize Bishop's writing — and *then* he gave me the Buddha, the Buddha he now wants back. I've come to the conclusion," she said crisply, "that Detwiler is quite innocent of betraying Carstairs and the Department."

"*What?*"

She nodded. "I think he deliberately sent wild reports during these past two months to draw Carstairs attention to him, and I believe he desperately hoped that someone would be sent to Hong Kong to investigate."

"You're kidding," said Robin.

She shook her head. "When I arrived he knew at once — from my asking for Sheng Ti, and from the memo with Bishop's writing on it — that I'd been sent by Carstairs."

Robin, frowning, said, "Then what—?"

"I think Detwiler is in very grave trouble," she said simply. "I wondered why I was followed only the one afternoon by the Man with the Attaché Case. I think now he wanted only to learn at what hotel I was staying because he *didn't dare be heard asking that.* The Man with the Attaché Case was Detwiler's man, and it was he whom Detwiler sent to burglarize my room the other night."

"As I know only too well," said Robin. "But for what purpose?"

"For the Buddha, of course," she said. "It took me far too long to see this because I was still assuming that Detwiler was completely in control at Feng Imports. He simply had to get the Buddha back, and when the burglary failed he was reduced to this morning's phone call to get it back. Nothing made sense until I began last night to shift all the facts around — juggling them, so to speak: the fact that Detwiler hadn't been at home for two months, which seemed inexplicable...the strangeness of that Monday morning visit to the shop... that ridiculous burglary...the fact that he and

Inspector Hao had been friends...Once I stopped viewing Detwiler as a traitor all the pieces fell into place and I realized the trouble he's in: Detwiler's being held prisoner — he's an unwilling victim — at Feng Imports."

Marko said, "Good God, are you suggesting—?"

She nodded. "Who but Mr. Feng? A little blackmail applied to Detwiler about his spying activities, the introduction of drugs to weaken his will and gain control — Sheng Ti was very positive about the drugs...It was important that Detwiler give me the Buddha openly, as an act of generosity, but I believe that under duress he's now been forced into admitting to Feng what he did, and it's been demanded of him that he get it back."

"By Mr. Feng," Robin said in astonishment.

She nodded. "Yes...What, after all, do any of us know of Mr. Feng?"

Marko said, "What do *you* know of Feng?"

"A shadow figure," she said. "A man who runs a shop that's a cover for Detwiler's intelligence-gathering activities. A man who gives the impression of being defeated by life, and resigned to life's passing him by, yet by the time I left the shop such an impression had completely vanished. I thought him cold and manipulative — shrewd, too, in the way he examined me — and hostile."

"But to be mixed up with *terrorists?*"

Mrs. Pollifax shrugged. "We simply don't know why yet, but — why not?"

Robin whistled. "Obviously immediate inquiries into Mr. Feng are in order, which I must say will be easier now that we've made personal contact with the special unit last night. But where does the Buddha fit in?"

"Very firmly," said Mrs. Pollifax. "If I'm right about Detwiler, then the Buddha is the only reason that he risked Feng's anger by overriding him and taking me into the back room — and if Feng is the supplier of his drugs then it was a reckless and very brave move on Detwiler's part. I think at some earlier stage of events, before he became so dependent on drugs, Detwiler had hopes of doing much more. When I arrived he was having one of his good days and he did what he could."

Walking over to the Buddha she picked it up and carried it to Robin. "There has to be something important about the Buddha for Detwiler to have gone to such lengths to give it to me. I hope it needn't be broken, it's so *very* lovely..."

"Good God," murmured Robin, staring at it and looking thoroughly jarred.

Leaning forward Marko said, "It would be more than one could hope, but — *mon Dieu,* if it has secrets—" He joined Robin on the couch, his fingers moving lightly over the figurine. "I would guess the headpiece, wouldn't you? It is the only part of the Buddha that does not look to have been carved out of the same piece of ivory." Drawing a pocketknife from his pocket he said, "Let *me.*"

Mrs. Pollifax winced as he inserted the knife at the base of the lacy headpiece. He applied pressure on the left side where it met the Buddha's shoulder, and then he removed the knife and applied pressure to the other side.

Abruptly, with a snapping sound, the headpiece was released from the clamplike tension that held it to the figure, and it flew to the floor.

"And there," she said proudly, pointing to the cavity carved into the head, "is Detwiler's hiding place. He *is* a friend."

"With something inside," Robin said softly.

"Yes," said Marko, and extracted four tiny slips of tightly rolled up paper. "The gods are smiling," he added as he flattened them out. After a glance at the first two he handed them to Mrs. Pollifax. "These I should not read; they appear to be the true reports Detwiler did not send to your superiors, and have something to do with foreign ships in Hong Kong harbor."

"But not this one," cried Robin, snatching up the third slip of paper. "Names, Marko, *names* − listen!" He read them aloud: "Eric Johansen − that's Eric the Red. Xian Pi − he's new. Charles Szabo − oh, we know him all right. Jan von Damm. John Yonomoto. Hoban Holloway − he's a killer, that one. Miguel Valentos, John D'Eon, Carl Eberhardt, Henri Duval and Angelo Gregorio."

"Eleven," nodded Mrs. Pollifax, "to match those eleven passports."

"The whole damn roster of the Liberation 80's group!" exclaimed Marko.

"But there's more − this is unbelievable," said Robin. "It has to be notes on their plan of attack."

Over his shoulder they peered at the last slip of paper:

1. The Tower/Peak. Command Center
2. Government House?
3. Radio station
4. Power station

Marko whispered, "So now we know... what a find! Mrs. P., we are in your debt."

"But still no mention of *when*," pointed out Mrs. Pollifax. "We're assuming the terrorists plan to take over Hong Kong by late next week, but only because Detwiler's housekeeper expects him home by then, and that's very tenuous, vague and secondhand and gives no clue at all as to what day."

"No, but we'll take no chances," said Robin, "I'll put through a call to the Governor at once — don't worry, he'll understand without my saying too much over the phone — and alert him to their *modus operandi.*" He went to the phone and began dialing.

Marko, smiling at Mrs. Pollifax, said, "So I think we now have a busy day finding out about this Mr. Feng of yours, among other matters. And you — what is this decision of yours to walk into the lion's den? You know the risk."

From the other side of the room, phone in hand, Robin said, "Risk? Suicidal! You're thinking of delivering an empty Buddha to Feng Imports, and you expect them to let you return here?"

"I'm not even considering the Buddha that Mr. Detwiler gave me," she said with dignity. "There's a very similar one down in the mall in a gift shop, inferior in workmanship but otherwise the same size, identical pose and carved from the same fine white ivory. Mr. Detwiler will see at once that it's not the same Buddha but I doubt that Mr. Feng will notice."

"Nonsense," growled Robin, and then his call came through and he turned his back on them, speaking in a low, rapid voice of what they'd just learned.

Marko pointed out gently, "Mr. Feng will know the difference once he attempts to open up a Buddha that cannot be opened."

"There are no terrorists at Feng Imports," she reminded him with a lift of her chin. "There'll be Detwiler and Mr. Feng, and Sheng Ti and Lotus in the building, and you have men watching both the front and the back of Feng Imports. If I can't defend myself against those odds—"

Robin, hanging up the phone, returned to them. "You've got to put this insane idea out of your head," he said flatly. "My God, woman, you must know it's too dangerous. If Mr. Feng is behind this he'll be waiting for you!"

"Of course," she said, nodding. "He was undoubtedly listening to every word Detwiler said to me on the phone, and holding a gun on Detwiler, too, for all I know."

"Then why?" demanded Robin.

She considered this, wondering if he would understand. She said at last, slowly, "Because if I *don't* go I think it quite possible that Detwiler will be killed for giving me the Buddha — his usefulness must certainly be coming to an end...Because Detwiler has been my assignment...Because his telephone call was an appeal for help...and because if I go, I just may learn from Detwiler the day and hour of the terrorist attack."

Robin said incredulously, "And you expect Feng to let you leave?"

With a glance at her wristwatch she said briskly, "I'll make every attempt, of course, to play the part of an innocent in all this but if it's necessary to use force I see no reason why my knowing a little karate should unduly raise Mr. Feng's suspicions. And as I pointed out earlier, you have Krugg and Upshot nearby, and Sheng Ti and Lotus already on the premises."

"If they all *stay* there," said Robin darkly.

Marko cleared his throat and spoke. "That is something you could double-check, then, before she goes, is it not?"

"My God," said Robin, turning on him, "you, too?"

Mrs. Pollifax stood up, saying dryly, "Robin, you're sounding more and more like an overprotective parent, you know there are no guarantees in this business. In the meantime I'm the only one given entree into — as Marko puts it — the lion's den, and I shall hope to discover something from Detwiler that may help to prevent eleven Liberation 80's men turning Hong Kong into another French hostage affair." She glanced at her watch. "If you can lend me three hundred Hong Kong dollars — for this, too, I need you," she said ruefully, "I'll go down and buy the other Buddha now, because it's already half-past ten and I promised to be at Feng Imports by eleven. The Buddha," she added, "costs a great deal of money and I've not enough at the moment and I absolutely refuse to give up this particularly glorious Buddha."

With an amused smile Marko brought out his wallet and counted bills into her hand. "I think we will be here when you return," he said. "*I* intend to be, yes, and in the meantime I will speak with Robin here most seriously."

She gave him a grateful smile. "Thanks." With a more ironic smile for Robin she waved and left.

When she returned twenty minutes later only Marko was in her room, eating the toast from her breakfast tray and sipping another cup of coffee. He took the Buddha from her and unwrapped it, holding it up next to the original, and he nodded. "Not bad!"

"Where's Robin?"

"Robin is speaking by radio to our two men in Dragon Alley, telling them that you will be coming. He's giving orders that at any sign of disturbance inside the shop after you've arrived they are to act at once. Of course he does not want to see you go," he added, "and for this you must be patient. He is newer at this game than you or I, and for you he has much fond-ness. He doesn't understand."

Mrs. Pollifax nodded.

"He has been persuaded," continued Marko, "but only because of this." He brought from his pocket an object somewhat smaller in size than the eraser at the end of a pencil. "For this," he said, "you will cut open a seam in the hem of your frock and insert it inside. It is a device to tell us where you are at all times. A — what do you say in English — homing signal. We call it an Ackameter."

"All right," said Mrs. Pollifax, and went to her suitcase for needle and thread and scissors. When the device had been sewn into her skirt she brought out the original wrappings in which the first Buddha had been placed, and carefully wrapped the imitation. With a glance at her watch, she made a face. "I'll just make it if I hurry."

Marko nodded. "Robin has double-checked — no one has left Feng Imports this morning."

"Good," she said, smiling at him. "Marko—" She held out her hand.

He clasped it warmly. "When Cyrus arrives I will speak to him about recruiting you for Interpol," he said humorously and then, con-tinuing to hold her hand he said gravely, "If ever I am in Detwiler's situation — may heaven forbid such a catastrophe — I shall fervently hope for a Mrs. Pollifax to ride to my rescue. Take care, Mrs. P.!"

"Thank you, Marko," she told him with equal gravity, and withdrawing her hand from his, she picked up the Buddha and left.

Capturing an elevator almost immediately she descended to the ground floor and walked to the front entrance for a taxi; the sun was in her eyes as she emerged from under the canopy and she held up a hand to signal for a cab. One of them pulled out of line and stopped in front of her, a door was opened for her and she had climbed inside before she saw that the cab already held a passenger.

"Oh — so sorry!" she murmured, making a move to withdraw, and then she recognized the occupant of the cab and realized that something had gone horribly wrong, dismally and horribly wrong.

"You are most punctual," said Mr. Feng with a faint dry smile. "Drive on, Carl — quickly, before we are noticed."

# 13

Robin was in their suite sitting by the radio when Marko joined him. "She's gone?" he said with a lift of one brow.

"She has just left, yes," confirmed Marko, and then, very gently, "Detwiler is her job, Robin, she had to do this. I am impressed — very."

Robin shook his head. "I still don't like it," he said. Leaning forward he flicked on the switch of the transmitter. "Raven here, are you reading me?"

Krugg's hearty voice replied. "Loud and clear, old chap."

"Our friend has just left the hotel. Start the alert and let me know as soon as she arrives."

"Got you, Raven, over and out."

Robin turned the dial slightly and called in Upshot at the warehouse behind Feng Imports. "Keep your line open," he told him. "Our party's just left the hotel and should be arriving you-know-where in about fifteen minutes."

"Right on," said Upshot.

Robin glanced at Marko and then at his watch. "Three minutes past eleven...she's wearing the Ackameter?"

Marko nodded and drew from his pocket a slightly larger disk than he'd given Mrs. Pollifax. Pressing a button he attached it by suction cup to the wall, where it gave out a steady insistent hum. "Working," he said. "Has Duncan reported yet on that radio-detection van?"

Robin nodded. "Good man, Duncan, the unit took to the streets at six this morning."

"Very efficient," murmured Marko. "Now which of us hunts out facts about Mr. Feng this morning?"

Robin gave him a quick smile. "I've been efficient too, I've already discussed this with Duncan and he promises a report on Mr. Feng by midafternoon, giving it top priority and complete secrecy. However," he added, "once Mrs. Pollifax completes her visit there's no reason why we can't do a bit of investigating ourselves."

Marko nodded. "She ought to be at Feng Imports in what, twenty minutes at the outside?"

Robin reached for the map of Hong Kong

and traced out the route. "Let's see...with no traffic possible in Dragon Alley she'll leave the cab at the street above and walk down..." He checked his watch again. "It's eleven-twelve now...Figuring a short wait for a taxi and even the worst of traffic, eleven-forty should do it." Looking up a call number on his memo pad he contacted the radio-detection van cruising the streets. "Radio One at Hong Kong Hilton," he said crisply. "We've sent out a party wearing an Ackameter, heading for the vicinity of Lower Lasar Row...If by chance you pick it up, ignore it, we've a line on it here."

A relieved voice said, "We're sure picking it up, it's been driving us bats. Mind giving us your ID so we know this is authentic?"

"Blue Dragon," said Robin with a sigh, feeling as usual like a child with these passwords.

"Thanks. Over and out."

Marko said, "Have a cup of coffee."

Robin nodded, left his chair, poured himself a cup and returned to the radio to switch it on. To Krugg he said, "Raven here, I'm changing over to Receiving and leaving the line open for you now."

Krugg said, "Roger...Nothing yet, all quiet."

Marko carried a chair closer to the radio and sat with one leg over its arm, relaxed and waiting. Robin envied his calm. He knew Marko's history, knew how hard-won was his detachment, but Robin conceded that he still found such calm impossible, he became too involved and now it was Mrs. Pollifax, his friend whom he had to worry about, and he felt ruffled and cross. He looked forward intensely to her arrival at Feng Imports, and he anticipated with even more fervor her safe departure from Feng Imports.

The Ackameter continued its steady drone and Robin's tension began to infect the room. At half-past eleven Krugg said, "Still nothing..." and Robin put down his coffee and began to pace the floor.

They had agreed that she would be there by eleven-forty; at eleven-forty Robin swore, went to the radio, switched it to transmitting and barked, "What's happening?"

"Nothing," replied Krugg.

"I'm switching you off but I'll be back." He quickly called the radio-detection van. "Blue Dragon," he said. "That homing signal – I want a reading on it at once, something may have gone wrong. Right away – and report back to Radio One." When he turned to Marko it was to give him a wan smile. "What do you think – a traffic jam, accident, flat tire – or trouble?"

Without replying Marko moved to the radio

and switched to Krugg's channel. "Don't take your eyes off the target," he said, "but give us a run-down on who's left the shop — if anyone — since Robin checked with you half an hour ago. Read me everything in your report. You've Witkowski's list there, too?"

"*Ja*...Let's see, when I came on duty the old Chinese chap was just entering the shop carrying one of those string bags with fruit in it. At eight the young man Sheng Ti entered, and forty minutes later the pretty girl — Lotus, is it? — and then—"

"Wait a minute, go back," said Marko. "If the 'old Chinese gentleman' entered at seven — Mr. Feng — when did he leave the shop?"

There was a silence and then Krugg said, "Damned if I know! I just looked over Witkowski's list — he went off duty at six-thirty, as you know — and there's no entry of the chap leaving."

Stunned, Robin broke in to say furiously, "Did Witkowski fall asleep? Damn it, why do they send us burnt-out agents fresh off another case? He *must* have fallen asleep, Feng had to leave the building somehow if he returned to it."

Krugg said flatly, "I've worked with Witkowski before and Witkowski doesn't fall asleep on the job."

Robin drew in his breath sharply. "My God," he said, "do you suppose there's another way out, another exit we missed?"

"Gently, gently," said Marko, and dialing the radio detection van he said quietly, "Radio One, Blue Dragon. Anything on the homing signal yet?"

"At the moment, sir, it appears to be stationary in the Man Mo Temple area," the man reported. "We're heading toward it now down Queen's Road Central and should be able to zero in on it inside of ten minutes at the most. Congested area."

"Thanks – keep in touch," said Marko, and turning to Robin, "That's reassuring, she's still in the Western District."

"I'm going," announced Robin, reaching for his jacket. "The Renault's still parked in the rear, I can get there as fast as the van, maybe even faster."

"Take your gun," said Marko quietly.

Robin whirled on him, glared and snarled, "Don't tell me that damn impervious optimism of yours has been dented slightly." He stopped and added stiffly, "Sorry, Marko, really I am."

"No harm done – fortunes of war," murmured Marko, and as Robin slid a gun into his holster he handed him the Ackameter's miniaturized detector, not as powerful as the apparatus installed in the van that was cruising the streets but a reliable gadget that would guide him to the Ackameter that Mrs. Pollifax was wearing. "I'll stay with the radio," he said, "and I'll double-check Upshot on the rear exit of Feng Imports."

Robin stopped with his hand on the knob of the door. He said in a strangled voice, "Detwiler and Feng are both supposed to be inside the shop — *inside it*, Marko, waiting for Mrs. Pollifax. If one of them left, somehow — if one of them left without our knowing—" He turned, opened the door and went out, slamming it behind him. A moment later he was racing down the hall to the freight elevator and presently he was risking a speeding ticket in the Renault, swearing at every traffic light, blowing his horn at every slow car, taking every short cut he could find.

Soon he was in one of the oldest, most crowded sections of Hong Kong, where the narrow streets gave him a dozen new frustrations until, spotting a rare parking space, he inched the car into it, jumped out and began to run. The Ackameter hummed confidently in the palm of his hand and the distance meter set into it clicked quietly, measuring the distance between it and the electronically-attuned mate that had been sewn into the hem of Mrs. Pollifax's skirt. As he turned the corner and hurried past the old Suzie Wong hotel he saw the red-and-gold façade of the Man Mo Temple beyond it, and the Ackameter's hum rose to a nearly hysterical pitch. Robin paused in confusion: there were no taxis in sight, and there was no sign of Mrs. Pollifax. As he stood there, an unmarked gray van pulled up to the ornate wall opposite the Temple and when a man in coveralls stepped out Robin crossed over to say quietly, "Special Unit?"

The man gave him a level stare. "Special *what?*"

"Radio One," he said. "Blue Dragon."

The man visibly relaxed. "ID?"

Robin pulled out a crumpled ID card from the concealed pocket in his jacket and said dryly, "I would think my Ackameter would be ID enough. Shall we move along before a crowd collects to see why I'm wired for sound?"

The man gave him a brief smile. "We've pinned down the location of the homing device to either inside or in back of the temple. I'm Harold Lei, by the way, and that's Jim Bai, who'll take the rear. Shall we go?"

They hurried into the temple, where Robin became aware of an ancient and extraordinary beauty — of brasses gleaming against clear bright scarlets, of incense-coils suspended from the ceiling like delicate hooded canopies – that would have pleased and soothed him if he'd not been feverishly looking for Mrs. Pollifax. And she was not here.

"Damn," he said aloud, eliciting a startled glance from the temple-keeper reading a newspaper in the corner.

They met outside again, the three of them.

"Nothing in the rear," reported Jim Bai. "What's happening with that Ackameter of yours?"

Robin glanced down at the distance meter and groaned. "Oh God," he said, the words wrung from him, *"it registers zero."*

"Then it has to be here," pointed out Harold Lei, frowning.

"You don't understand–" began Robin, wanting to shout at him that the Ackameter was being carried by a woman, and the woman should be here. He abandoned his protest when he saw Harold Lei bend down and pick up what looked to be a pebble at their feet.

"This it?" he said.

As it was dropped into the palm of his hand Robin felt an acute sense of despair. "So they've got her," he said bitterly. "Too smart for us again, and my God what an insult to deliberately leave this here for us. Except–" But he didn't finish his thought; he didn't want to remember that the disk had been sewn into Mrs. Pollifax's skirt, which meant there would have been a threat of violence, or violence itself, to separate it from her. "I need a phone," he told Harold. "I've got to call your superior, this changes things."

"In the van – direct connection," Lei told him.

Briefly Robin delivered the news of Mrs. Pollifax's abduction to Duncan, head of the Special Unit, the man to whom the Governor had introduced him with every assurance of his probity.

"Now what did she want to do that for," the man said calmly. "Damn awkward, this. Blows everything sky high if they apply pressure and she tells them all we know."

"Which isn't all that much," Robin said darkly.

"Enough to alter their plans, and we do know something of those now."

"Yes – thanks to Mrs. Pollifax," he reminded him angrily.

"Where are you now?"

"Man Mo Temple, about to head back to the hotel."

"Good. Tell my men to get back on the job and I'll talk with you later. And – steady, old chap!"

"Yes," was all that Robin managed to say, while inside of him he raged at all that was abruptly going wrong, at his fears for Mrs. Pollifax, and at himself for lacking the sureness to have absolutely forbidden her to go. Which, he conceded miserably, would never have succeeded anyway, not with Mrs. Pollifax.

Cutting the connection he exchanged a few words with the two men and then walked to the Renault and drove somberly back to the hotel. This time he didn't bother to cover his tracks by taking the freight elevator; if anyone was still interested in following him, he thought grimly, he'd welcome the chance to thrust them against a wall, put a gun to their head and demand that he be taken to Mrs. Pollifax. Only direct action could blunt the realization that they'd been outmaneuvered again and Mrs. Pollifax captured, and in his head there lingered the words *if they apply pressure and she tells them all we know*...

Pressure...a tactful word for torture, of course.

As he reached the bank of elevators in the lobby a down elevator opened its door and Mr. Hitchens and Ruthie walked out.

"Rob — Lars!" cried Mr. Hitchens happily, recovering the name in time. "Oh, do meet Ruthie, this is — *Something's wrong*," he said, staring at Robin.

Robin nodded. "They've got Mrs. Pollifax." He saw that Mr. Hitchens was involved enough to look stricken by his words and he felt an odd sense of comfort from this.

"*They,*" faltered Mr. Hitchens. "You mean—"

"Yes."

"Oh dear!"

Ruthie said, "But I saw her only an hour or so ago, what's happened?"

"Saw her?" Robin said, turning to her in surprise. "Where? When?"

"She was getting into a taxi at the front entrance," Ruthie told him.

Robin laid a hand on her shoulder. "Let's try that couch over there," he said grimly, "I want to hear this." Once seated he said, "Talk!"

Ruthie nodded. "I was strolling up the curved walk toward the entrance and I saw Mrs. Pollifax walk out through the glass doors. I think the sun must have been in her eyes for she shielded them for a minute, and then she dropped her hand and lifted the other to wave at one of the cabs waiting, and when the cab moved up she climbed inside. It was about a minute before eleven and I didn't call out to her because I was meeting Hitch at eleven, and I was late."

"All right, now let me ask you, Ruthie: was it

a bonafide taxi that she climbed into?"

Ruthie looked startled. "You mean that's when she disappeared? Oh dear, let me think... Well — she was standing there, waiting, the sun in her eyes — yes, she was squinting a little, and the cab—" She stopped. "That's funny. As I walked up the drive there were three taxis waiting for a passenger but it was another one, coming from where I don't know, that suddenly pulled up to Mrs. Pollifax."

"What did it look like?"

She frowned. "Well — red. Like the others. A light on top."

"Was there anyone inside it but the driver?"

Ruthie closed her eyes for a second. "Yes," she said in a startled voice. "Yes, I could see the silhouette of a person sitting in the rear, and — and then Mrs. Pollifax's head, too, as she climbed inside and then — yes, I saw her head jerk back, as if she'd just noticed the cab was occupied and was going to back out. But the taxi started up in a hurry and drove away with her in it." She opened her eyes. "Will she be all right?" she asked anxiously.

"That," said Robin, "is something only Mr. Hitchens can tell us, but at the moment I've got to hurry back upstairs and set a great many things in motion. And thanks, Ruthie — this may be of some help."

With this he entered the elevator to return to a waiting Marko and tell him the grim news.

Krugg came off duty at 4 P.M. and fell into bed to sleep for a few hours.

Witkowski left his bed to replace him until midnight.

A taxi reported stolen in the Causeway Bay area at ten o'clock that morning was found at three o'clock, abandoned on Hennessy Road.

Even more important, reports began to filter in during the afternoon on Mr. Charles Yuan Feng, the owner of Feng Import Company, 31½ Dragon Alley, and all of them were extremely interesting.

He had a police dossier. According to this dossier he had come to Hong Kong from Shanghai after serving in an unknown capacity under Generalissimo Chiang Kai Shek; he had been accompanied by a brother, Weng Feng. At this time — it was in the 1950s — one or both of the brothers was suspected of having connections with the "14-K" triad, which the Nationalist General Koi Sui-heong had brought with him as a legacy from China, resurrecting it in Hong Kong for the purpose of overthrowing Mao and returning the Nationalists to mainland China.

In 1967 the brother Weng Feng had been

arrested in Hong Kong as a Nationalist spy and saboteur, the police having found an arsenal of weapons in his apartment. In 1968 Weng had been quietly deported to Taiwan, where he still lived, and it had been assumed that he was the troublemaker of the family.

Following this, interest in Mr. Charles Yuan Feng had lessened, and then had been dropped, although his name remained on a list.

Robin scowled over the report unhappily. "Does it mean anything or doesn't it? I mean, Hong Kong is *full* of Nationalist refugees. Nationalists' Day is still celebrated in October — the Double Ten — and amateur conspiracies are still occasionally surfacing."

"But this is no amateur conspiracy," pointed out Marko. "It's difficult to make any connection at all."

Robin nodded. "It seems inconceivable, and yet Britain and Peking are meeting right now — again — it's in today's newspaper — negotiating the terms under which Hong Kong will be returned to the Chinese in 1997." He frowned. "And it's to Red China the colony's to be returned, not to the Nationalists, as once envisioned." His frown deepened. "I daresay it could make for a bit of rage, seeing Hong Kong — the capitalist center of the Orient — being turned over to a country of communes and communism."

"But Eric the Red and the Liberation 80's group?" said Marko skeptically.

There was no answer to that, but there was one interesting footnote in the dossier that dangled possibilities of a Nationalist connection: Mr. Feng's brother, the deported Nationalist spy, had been married to a woman by the name of Xian Sutsung, and the list discovered in Mrs. Pollifax's Buddha had included a Xian Pi.

*Nephew?* wondered Robin as he went downstairs for an early dinner in the restaurant, leaving Marko behind to man the radio until his return. It proved nothing except that Chinese could join terrorist movements, too, but still it was interesting. To him personally it seemed an aeon ago that Chiang Kai Shek had been routed out of mainland China to set up his new government on Taiwan. Chiang Kai Shek was long since dead; Mao, too, had gone, yet Robin knew only too well how old conflicts and rivalries could linger and fester; history was full of them as new boundaries were carved out of old wars, with no regard for sects, nationalities or alliances: Tatars against Turks, Sikh against Hindu, Serbs against Croats, Druzeans against Christians...And certainly Taiwan was still insisting — decades later —

that it was the only true government of China.

Robin glanced at his watch as he entered the hotel dining room; it was a few minutes after six and he realized how drained he felt by the events of the day; he couldn't even remember when he'd last eaten, and he began to understand Marko's insistence that he leave the radio for an hour. He headed for a table in the corner, fitted neatly against the wall, and seated himself, unfurling the napkin folded at his place.

Three tables away he saw the flutter of a hand: Ruthie and Mr. Hitchens were trying to catch his attention, both of them smiling and waving.

Ruthie leaned forward now and called, "You look exhausted so we won't join you, but has Mrs. Pollifax been found yet?"

Fortunately there were few diners at this hour to hear her indiscretion. Robin forced his lips into a polite smile and shook his head.

At the table next to him along the wall a man facing Robin glanced from him to Ruthie and rose from his chair: a large man, in a somewhat rumpled suit, with an intelligent face, sleepy eyes and a thatch of white hair. To Robin's astonishment, he walked over to his table, pulled out a chair and sat down.

"Believe I just heard my wife's name," he said, giving Robin a searching and interested scrutiny. "Flew in two hours ago and nobody can find her...Emily Pollifax?"

"Good God," cried Robin, shocked out of his lethargy, "you're Cyrus Reed and it's Thursday!"

"Yes to both," he said, and added calmly, "Take it Emily's gone and put herself in the thick of things again. Always does...Don't have the slightest idea who you are, but it looks as if I've arrived just in the nick of time... Now what are you doing about finding my wife?"

# 14

Mrs. Pollifax, finding herself in the taxi with Mr. Feng, decided that discretion was the better part of valor: holding back the dismay that gripped her she forced her lips into a polite and expectant smile, as if Detwiler had very graciously sent a cab for her and had included Mr. Feng as a special treat. Actually she could think of nothing to say anyway, nothing at least that wouldn't betray or incriminate her, such as how on earth had he managed to leave Feng Imports without Robin and Marko knowing, and where was Mr. Detwiler?

"I do try to be punctual," she told him, repressing every normal reaction. "I feel it's a courtesy to others, don't you?"

This conversational gambit was ignored, as she had supposed it would be. They were leaving Queen's Road Central now and turning into a narrow street distinctly Chinese in character; as the taxi slowed Mr. Feng leaned forward, pointed and the car halted in front of a narrow shop with the sign TAILOR hung above it.

It was now that Mr. Feng chose to remove a small gun from his sleeve, and at sight of it Mrs. Pollifax gave him a reproachful glance. She would have much preferred to go on avoiding reality for a little longer, she simply wasn't ready yet to confront the fact that she'd walked into a trap — one needed time to adjust to such matters, she thought — but of course the gun made this impossible.

"Out — quickly," he told her in his quiet voice. "Leave the Buddha on the seat, we have five minutes, no more."

Five minutes for what, Mrs. Pollifax wondered, but since no opportunity was presenting itself to flee she placed the package on the seat and allowed herself to be prodded through the open door of the tailor shop, considerably confused as to what Feng had in mind. It was a small shop; there was a man at a steam iron, four women seated at sewing machines basting sleeves into silk jackets, and two curtained dressing rooms. No one seemed surprised to see either Mr. Feng or Mrs. Pollifax; without so much as a word or a smile one of the women rose from her bench and went to stand beside one of the dressing rooms. She had a sullen, hard face and regarded Mrs. Pollifax without curiosity.

"You will strip," said the woman.

"I will *what?*" said Mrs. Pollifax incredulously.

"Quickly," she said. "Everything."

Obviously she had been expected, and if she demurred there was Mr. Feng's gun pressing into her back. Mrs. Pollifax went into the stall and stripped, handing out her clothing piece by piece; when this had been done the woman entered the cubicle and subjected Mrs. Pollifax to an aggressive and not too gentle body search.

*Well,* thought Mrs. Pollifax bleakly, *this is happening in obscure corners of the world every day and probably every hour, and it's only right that I experience it to know how it feels. And how it feels,* she thought with rising anger, *is humiliating.* When it was over her clothes were handed back to her piece by piece, and without surprise Mrs. Pollifax found the homing device in the hem of her skirt gone. It was for this, then, that they'd made their stop, and as she was herded back into the car she thought of Krugg still waiting in Dragon Alley for her arrival, and of Robin and Marko presumably still listening for the sound of her Ackameter, which would now be sending out signals from a tailor shop.

228

But in this she was wrong, as she discovered when the taxi came to a stop in sight of the Man Mo Temple and Mr. Feng drew out the tiny electronic device and placed it in the palm of the driver's hand. The man he called Carl left the taxi and she had to sit and watch him deposit the Ackameter at the entrance to the temple while she thought over and over, *Damn, they've thought of everything — everything!*

It was at this moment that Mrs. Pollifax opened herself up to the reality of her situation and let it sweep over her with all of its monstrous implications: she had walked into a trap, but *not* the cozy little trap that she'd envisioned at Feng Imports, with Sheng Ti and Lotus nearby, and Krugg across the lane and Upshot watching in the rear. She was now in the hands of the terrorists, with all earthly help in the guise of Robin, Marko, Carstairs and the police denied her. She was completely on her own, destination unknown, outcome so uncertain that she did not feel any insurance company would consider her life expectancy a safe risk against such odds.

And Cyrus was on his way...but she mustn't think of Cyrus because under duress she was going to have to be very careful not to expose what she knew, and in this area Cyrus would be a distraction, representing all the delightful normalities of life that she loved and wanted very much to continue. She must, for instance, keep Mr. Feng and his friends from discovering that Interpol was involved, that Eric the Red had been seen in Hong Kong and identified, and above all that radio detection vans cruised the street now, listening for a signal from their transmitter.

*I have to stay aware,* she thought, *I have to keep my wits about me.*

They had been negotiating narrow congested streets, sometimes forced to halt for crowds of pedestrians, street stalls and hawkers and trucks. Once in these labyrinthian lanes she thought they might be very close to Dragon Alley, but they were certainly in a very old section of Hong Kong where only Chinese lived, and a great many of them.

Abruptly Carl turned to the right into a lane scarcely wide enough for the taxi; he stopped, reached over and opened Mr. Feng's door and a minute later Mr. Feng, still with gun, opened the opposite door to Mrs. Pollifax. She glanced once at his face, at the creped parchment of his skin, the benign and hooded eyes set too close together and she thought, *Yon Cassius has a lean and hungry look, he thinks too much . . .* but of what? What passion behind those inscrutable eyes had led him to this?

She climbed out of the car to face a battered, faded-blue wooden door. The taxi backed out of the lane, Mr. Feng held open the wooden door for her to enter, and even as she moved toward him she was calculating distance and strike possibilities, but he was too clever for her, moving adroitly out of reach as she passed him. Faced with steps and a gun behind her Mrs. Pollifax began to climb dark, narrow, tilting stairs that continued endlessly. No voice or sounds could be heard behind the few narrow doors she passed on the three minuscule landings; when she reached the top of the building a door opened and light spilled over the shabby floor and into her face, nearly blinding her after the dim halls.

"Take her," Mr. Feng told the man who opened the door, and turned and went back down the stairs.

Blinking, Mrs. Pollifax stared into the face of the man confronting her and decided, quite reasonably, that she didn't like it, resenting especially his look of Nordic wholesomeness. He was blond, clean-shaven and tanned and she thought he looked like any Hong Kong vacationer in his cotton turtleneck shirt, jeans and sandals except that he was wearing a gun-belt and levelling a gun at her, his eyes like cold hard blue marbles. She was pulled inside to enter a room crammed full of people and objects illuminated by brilliant fluorescent lighting overhead. The scene was chaotic: windows had been covered over with yellowing newspapers, sleeping bags lay everywhere, some of them occupied, and piles of cable lay on the floor like coiled snakes. Along one wall she saw rows of bottles and jars, a metal drum, a barrel, an assortment of wooden crates. At the far end of the room two men were using a blowtorch, their goggles turning them into Martians, the sparks flying to the ceiling. Three others were mixing and stirring something in a metal drum while two men leaned over what looked to be a radio, scowling and pointing and arguing. The heat in the room was stifling; her nose wrinkled at the smells of hot grease, rotting garbage, sweat and something pungent that she thought might be gasoline and fervently hoped not.

The gun prodded her toward the left wall; she moved past a wooden crate and abruptly stopped, seeing with a mixture of dismay and relief that she was not to be alone. Two other guests had preceded her and were sitting on the floor, their wrists tightly bound together in front of them: Detwiler, and a young man whose face she recognized at once from the newspapers: it was Alec Hao.

As she rounded the corner Detwiler lifted his head and gave her a wan smile, half apologetic, half rueful.

"Good morning — or afternoon," she said politely, and while she suffered her wrists to be bound with ropes — so tightly that unwilling tears came to her eyes — she kept her gaze resolutely on Alec Hao.

Once she was bound, the blond young man shoved her to the floor and she fell between Alec Hao and Detwiler, hitting her head against the wall in the plunge. Turning away with contempt the man strode off to another section of the room where she could see his head over the tops of the crates until he disappeared from view.

Detwiler turned his head to look at her. She said nothing — her head hurt and she wanted very much to rub it but of course she couldn't — and it was not until she noticed the tears in his eyes that she spoke. "I'm sorry," she told him softly.

"I can't think why," he said, struggling for dignity. "After all, I'm the one who — made the phone call. It was—" His voice trailed away shakily. "You brought the Buddha? Feng has it now?"

Mrs. Pollifax hesitated and then temporized by saying, "A Buddha, yes."

He groaned. "They'll kill me now they have it. You couldn't know — didn't — but it has a compartment inside — with plans — papers — as much as I knew, and — and—"

The ache where she'd struck her head was subsiding. She said in a neutral voice, "Just why did you want me to have the Buddha with its compartment and the papers inside, Mr. Detwiler?"

He shook his head. "I thought — I really thought that — at the right moment, you understand, I would telephone you — at your hotel — and tell you about it. Tell you what I'd hidden inside. I thought—" His nose was running and tears were returning to his eyes; with his tied wrists he dabbed ineffectually at his wet face.

Beside her Alec Hao said in a tired voice, "He's running out of dope, they gave him more last night to keep him quiet — he was screaming his head off — but that's a long time ago now. He needs a fix."

She had been right about the drugs, then, and obviously Detwiler was to be of no help. She was abruptly realizing, too, that in removing the papers from Mr. Detwiler's Buddha she had given him an unexpected gift, and herself a great deal of trouble, for when it was discovered that her Buddha didn't contain Detwiler's papers the attention would at once shift from him to her. She sighed over the most deadly error that she'd ever made: the supposition that she would be taken to the import shop. Why hadn't she and Robin and Marko copied out the contents of those plans Detwiler had made? It would have been assumed, then, that she was only an innocent bystander but, by substituting another Buddha she had in effect exposed and condemned herself, and it would be she who was questioned and pressured. It was not a pleasant thought, not when it would be terrorists who would be doing the questioning. . .

She said to him, "You knew when we met who I was, and why I was here?"

Detwiler nodded miserably.

"Does Mr. Feng know this too?"

A sob escaped him. "Probably – I don't know – don't know *what* I've told him. He began – I think he said he began with small amounts of drugs in my food – at the shop, at lunch – months ago. And then – after a while I scarcely knew what was wrong, things blurred, and then he told me – told me–" He lifted his bound hands to his face and wept. "Told me I was part of his plan – and that's when he brought out the needles and said I couldn't go home." He drew up his knees and leaned his head forward, gulping down sobs and shivering.

Looking at him Mrs. Pollifax tried to remember the suave and immaculate Detwiler she'd met on Monday, only four days ago, the man who had coolly asserted himself with Mr. Feng and had given her the Buddha. For weeks he must have been drifting back and forth between that man and this one, she thought, depending always on Mr. Feng for his rational moments. There were no gold cuff links or black silk suit today, the sandals he wore were torn and the cotton pants and shirt were wrinkled. She thought of his elegant house, of the elegant dinner parties that Mrs. O'Malley had described and she felt a stab of compassion for the wreck of a man beside her.

Alec Hao leaned forward to say accusingly, "Who are you, anyway? I heard you, I heard *him.*"

With a sense of relief she turned away from Detwiler. "I'm Emily Pollifax, and I believe you're Alec Hao?"

He looked at her with astonishment. "How —?"

"From your picture in the newspapers — Mr. Hitchens has been very worried about you."

"Hitchens! You know him? Did they get him too? Has he found my father yet?" His voice was eager but suspicion lingered in his eyes.

Bruises had turned his left cheekbone purple, his lips were swollen and one of his front teeth had been chipped, but he was young and resilient and he merely looked like a college boy who had emerged from a boxing match that had gone on for too long. But there was also anger in Alec Hao, the kind of anger that Detwiler had been incapable of sustaining, she thought, and this had preserved him so that she felt he could deal with the truth. She said gently, "Your father's dead, Alec."

He drew a long shuddering sigh, swallowed hard and nodded. "I guess I'm not surprised — not now. I think I stopped hoping three days ago. I mean, I'm surprised that I'm alive myself after being here three days." His voice trembled. "Did they — was it fast?"

"Fast and I think unexpected," she told him, keeping her voice low and calm. "He looked — surprised. It was a bullet in the temple." Leaning closer she added, "They had planned it to look like suicide; there was a scrap of paper with his writing on it, and the gun placed in his hand, but I removed them both."

"You *saw* him?" he said, astonished.

She nodded. "Mr. Hitchens and I found him — the next morning — in the same hut where you were captured. Mr. Hitchens and I flew in on the same plane from San Francisco," she explained, "and we had breakfast together, and so when he came back from the hut that night he was badly hurt and came to my room for help."

"Then you're a — a friend," he said in surprise. "Not that it makes any difference now, but still—"

"I know."

"*He* used to be," Alec said bitterly, with a jerk of his head toward Detwiler. "He knew my father and they were friends but they got to him, Mr. Feng and these people. Don't trust him, you mustn't."

"In the shape he's in now, no one could trust him," she said simply. "I do think, though, that he's tried to do his best against frightening odds."

He snorted at this. "You know him?"

"We — uh — have mutual friends," she said, "which is why I called on him Monday, after reaching Hong Kong. But you—" With a quick smile she changed this subject. "They've been rough on you here?"

"Sort of," he said with an attempt at a smile, "but it's over now. They plan to take over Hong Kong, did you know that? I laughed when I heard it but I'm not laughing any more." He jerked his head in the direction of the activity just beyond the wooden crates. "Know what they're mixing over there?"

She shook her head.

"Potash and diesel fuel. Plain old potash and diesel fuel you can get anywhere – it makes bombs. Last night they went out with explosives they planted somewhere in the city. From what I overheard, the bombs have long-term fuses that'll go off at different times over the next two and three days. They lower things out of those two windows over there, to a van they've hidden in the alley below. The windows are built so they can be lifted out easily. I suppose they're terrorists, aren't they?"

She nodded. "The Liberation 80's Group."

"*What?*" He looked staggered. "You mean *that's* what my dad stumbled into? My God, no wonder–" He shuddered. "No wonder, no wonder!"

"But Mr. Feng's the head man, isn't he?"

Alec looked at her in surprise. "That old man who wanders in and out? I've seen him dole out money once or twice, but what would Liberation 80's want with *him?*"

There was no ready answer to that, and Mrs. Pollifax turned back to Detwiler. Placing her tied wrists on his arm she leaned close to him. "Mr. Detwiler," she said, "can you hear me?"

He looked up, his eyes glazed, lips trembling.

"Mr. Feng," she said. "What does he want?"

For a moment Detwiler looked as if he neither saw nor heard her and then with an effort he steadied himself, but still his words came out in gasps. "Worked – slaved – for years he said." He stopped to wet his lips. "A bloody f-f-fanatic – and I never knew. One big suicidal – kamikaze." He gave up and lifted his bound hands over his head in a clumsy description of exploding fireworks. "Because Peking government – not legal. Only Taiwan. *Nationalists.*"

She looked at him in amazement and then she said, "How stupid and how cruel," and turned back to Alec. "Do you happen to have any idea when they plan this takeover of Hong Kong?"

"Oh yes," he said, "it's set for tomorrow morning. Around seven."

It was her turn to be staggered. "*Tomorrow?*" she gasped, stunned by this news. "Tomorrow morning...you mean Friday?"

He shrugged. "I don't even know what today is."

"Thursday," she told him automatically.

"Okay, then it's Friday or whatever tomorrow is."

"But that leaves us no time!" she cried.

"For what?" he asked in surprise.

"For stopping them. For getting out of here."

He looked at her incredulously. "Stopping them? Are you mad? There's nothing we can do, look at us. Look at *them.*"

She *was* looking, and hearing, too. Funny sounds of static were coming from a collection of tubes and wires linked to a black box that held a kinship to Robin's radio at the hotel. One of the welders strolled over to the box that was sitting some ten or twelve feet away from her in the next aisle, and when he removed his goggles she saw that it was Eric the Red. She watched him flick on a switch, pick up a pair of earphones and as he listened he turned and stared at Mrs. Pollifax.

She did not appreciate his singling her out with those cold empty eyes, and she felt a chill of foreboding.

Abruptly he put down the headpiece, flicked off the switch and walked down the aisle to her. Stopping in front of her, towering over her, he stared down at her and then he slapped her hard across her right cheek. "The Buddha was the wrong one," he said coldly in accented English. "*Not* the one you were given by Detwiler."

Beside her Mrs. Pollifax felt a sudden movement from Detwiler as Eric the Red's words penetrated his misery. Detwiler had turned his head to stare at her in astonishment, and with a dawning hope for himself.

Eric the Red reached down, seized her by the

shirt and dragged her to her feet. "We will see how much you know and what you did with the papers inside that statue."

Mrs. Pollifax thought bleakly, *It begins now*...and she prayed for strength as he dragged her out of the room.

# 15

It was half-past seven when Robin and Marko had finished describing to Cyrus the sequence of events and discoveries that had led to this hour. They were a somber trio as they sat near the silent radio in Robin's suite, surrounded by empty coffee cups and maps. There had been a moment, Robin noticed, when Cyrus turned white, but he'd rallied and remained calm, continuing to weigh facts as they were presented to him and questioning them as judiciously as if he still occupied his judge's bench. Robin could see that Marko was impressed, as was he: Cyrus was going to be all right; he might even prove to be a rock, and if so, thought Robin dryly, a very *large* rock, for it had not taken him long to see that Cyrus's six feet four inches of bulk held no fat, and that his air of drowsiness, his economical manner of speaking, concealed a mind that was quick and keen.

"So we're not in the best of shape," concluded Robin reluctantly. "This takeover of the Colony appears to have been painstakingly plotted over a long period of time. It's gained that kind of momentum that well-laid plans do acquire, until we've come to feel rather like gnats buzzing around a juggernaut. We can only tell you that Mrs. Pollifax disappeared at eleven o'clock this morning, and we guess now that it was Mr. Feng who occupied the taxi she entered because he walked back into his shop at twelve-fifteen, and it's a sample of our frustration that we hadn't even known that he'd left his shop."

"Following which," added Marko, "the radio-detection van reported a high-powered one-minute transmission from that approximate area, not long enough to be traced, but we're guessing it came from Feng Imports. Of Detwiler there's been no sign at all."

Cyrus nodded. "And you've not discovered how this Mr. Feng has come and gone from Feng Imports without your knowing of it? Does he suspect he's being watched?"

Robin hesitated. "We're fairly certain he hasn't spotted his surveillants," he said slowly. "At least we feel there are a number of things he could do if he suspected this, and he's done none of them. The first time he left it was in the dark of night, and since there are almost no lights in the alley we assumed he was just lucky. But of course he very obviously went out this morning – obviously, since we saw him come back – so that blew our comforting theory. Marko's working on the theory that he may have access to one or two adjacent buildings and have set up an escape route for the terrorists that he occasionally uses himself. Marko's sent out a query as to who owns the building next the shop. We're in touch now, you see, with a hand-picked group from Hong Kong special unit, but–"

"How many?" interrupted Cyrus.

"Seven," put in Marko. "Seven plus Duncan the head man."

"–but tracing landlords in Hong Kong is a very complicated business," finished Robin, "and on the subject of those seven hand-picked policemen I can't tell you how severely handicapped we've felt by not knowing whom to trust. We dare not take risks in that area! There's one route we prefer not to take, and that's to call in the press and publicize the situation. This might save Hong Kong – a happy issue – but we're very much afraid the Liberation 80's group would find the means and the contacts to be smuggled out of Hong Kong – there has to be some connection with the Triad here – and six months from now they'd only surface in another corner of the globe to work their deviltry. As members of an international police organization—" He shook his head. "You understand the responsibility, I'm sure. We want to not only recover Mrs. Pollifax but abort their mission and capture every damn member of the group and put them out of commission forever."

"And how much do you feel they know about your involvement?" pressed Cyrus.

Marko said gently, "If Mrs. Pollifax was accurate in her guesses of the situation, they would have known absolutely nothing until Detwiler confessed about the Buddha and what he'd concealed inside of it. Following this they would have understood that Mrs. Pollifax had — er — connections with Detwiler's intelligence-gathering activities, although Mr. Feng *may* have guessed this from the beginning."

"And now?" Cyrus's voice was even.

Marko spread out his hands in a gesture of helplessness. "We do not know."

"You mean it will be up to Emily."

Robin suddenly found it more comfortable to avoid Cyrus's eyes and to look at the floor.

Without expression Cyrus said, "All right, I think I've got the picture. Like to hear now what you're planning — you do have plans," he said tactfully, with the lift of an eyebrow. "You still have Feng Imports under surveillance?"

Marko nodded. "Yes, now that the — how do you say it, the cat is out of the sack, but yes. Also — at our request — the Governor has asked that regular police begin a door-to-door search for two missing English tourists, last reported" — he pointed to the map — "in the area where Mr. Hitchens targeted some activity. Or disturbing vibrations," he added dryly.

"Those two mythical tourists being part of the frustration," commented Robin. "We simply can't chance an informer getting word to Detwiler or Feng that Interpol is involved and so we have to come up with these ridiculous subterfuges."

Cyrus said pointedly, "They'll know something's up when they examine Emily's Buddha, won't they?"

This was met with an uncomfortable silence.

"You understand it's my wife they've captured," Cyrus pointed out dryly. "My impression is, you're not doing enough. Walking on eggs. Tied up in knots, damn it. You need manpower."

"Agreed," said Robin.

Cyrus nodded. "Then, damn it, if you can't

trust the police call in the Army, the British have soldiers stationed here, haven't they? Ask for a platoon, a squad, whatever the British call a detail. Use 'em. Position them. Not likely *they've* been bribed."

Robin whistled. "If it could be done!" he said with longing, and then, "It can scarcely help Mrs. Pollifax, though."

Cyrus gave him a steady look. "Don't know what *can* help Emily just now, do you? No fool Emily, she'll do all she can...Been in tight spots before. A little luck and we'll find her — that radio-detection van, perhaps, or one of those regular police knocking on the right door. Can't count on it, though. Best hope is they'll save her for a hostage."

Robin thought to himself that if that was their best hope it was a pretty damn feeble one because Mrs. Pollifax might be a captive of the terrorists for days — an entire week — and there was no knowing what might happen to her in the meantime.

"For myself," said Marko, "I am stricken by apologies that I wish to express. Robin and I have been feeling sorry for ourselves here in our dismay at this event, and it is you who gives the perspective, you who go at once to the heart and return us to action. Robin, go at once and call His Excellency and ask for soldiers."

"Right," said Robin, springing to his feet, and strode into the next room to make his call.

Half an hour later, when he returned to the living room, he found Marko introducing Cyrus to Mr. Hitchens and Ruthie. "We just couldn't enjoy ourselves," Mr. Hitchens was earnestly explaining to Cyrus. "Not while your wife's still missing, so we decided to come and see what's happening."

Marko turned to Robin. "What's happening is what I want to hear from Robin. You reached the Governor?"

Robin made a face. "Yes, but it took ages to track him down, he's at a dinner party and the connection was ghastly — all chitter-chatter and music in the background — but I think he caught the message. He's calling us back later . . . If I understood him correctly, with that foul connection we had, the calling out of the Army, even a handful of men, has to go through one or two channels."

"And what the hell does that mean?" inquired Cyrus with an edge to his voice.

Ruthie said, "He's appointed by the Queen, do you suppose he has to consult with *her?*"

"Doubtful," said Marko. "I believe there's an Executive Council, it could be that, and of course it's a damnably awkward hour of the night to contact anyone." With a charming smile he said, "Why don't we all sit down? I will call room service and while it is not necessary that we talk we can at least eat, and as you can see we have many chairs and couches here."

Ruthie, giving Cyrus a warm smile, said, "What it amounts to, you know, is that misery appreciates company. How are you doing, Cyrus?"

"Tolerably well," Cyrus said, but Robin noticed how tired he looked, and felt a stab of compassion.

As the others moved away, Marko held back Mr. Hitchens to ask in a low voice, "Would it be of help to Cyrus if you used your talents to reassure him?"

"Dear God no," blurted out Mr. Hitchens. "I've tried — I really tried...She's in a small dark room, and there's a man—" His voice trembled. "I couldn't continue; it's terribly unprofessional of me, but you see I *know* her, which makes such a difference. But things are *not* going well for her."

"I understand you," Marko said quietly, and releasing his arm, he moved to the telephone to call room service.

At ten o'clock Sheng Ti telephoned Robin, having been unable to reach Mrs. Pollifax in room 614. "You still have that taxi money?" asked Robin. "Good — hop into a cab and come at once to the Hilton Hong Kong's front entrance, I'll meet you there."

When Sheng Ti was brought into the suite, it was obvious that he was in shock from hearing of Mrs. Pollifax's disappearance, because he scarcely noticed the luxury into which he was thrust, and impatiently shook his head at the food offered him. Learning that Cyrus was Mrs. Pollifax's husband he went at once to him, fervently shook his hand and sat down close beside him on the couch as if he were the closest connection to Mrs. Pollifax that he could find.

But Sheng Ti had little to report, and little that they didn't already know, except for the fact that Mr. Detwiler had not been seen in the shop all day — which had never happened before — and Mr. Feng had spent many hours up in his rooms above the store, but when those hours were pinpointed they turned out to match the times that Mr. Feng had mysteriously vanished from the building. He and Lotus, he said, had been left in charge of the shop all day, working so hard to package a backlog of orders that Lotus had gone early to bed, exhausted.

"I stay," he announced. "I want you find Mrs. Poll'fax, please, she my friend from Turfan — from *China.*"

Cyrus reached over and patted his hand.

251

"You stay," he told him.

At eleven o'clock a call came through from Duncan in the special unit, reporting that Donald Chang, to whom Sheng Ti had delivered diamonds, had been quietly arrested at the airport. He appeared to know nothing of any terrorist plans; he'd been bribed to separate and remove certain marked crates and packages that arrived by air, thus circumventing their inspection by Customs. He had believed them to be diamonds on which Mr. Feng preferred not to pay duty. There was still nothing, Duncan added, from the regular police who were searching for the two mythical lost tourists.

At midnight Krugg reported no activity at Feng Imports and the building dark, and at quarter-past the hour the radio-detection van reported no transmitting activity.

By one o'clock the suite had begun to acquire the look of an encampment. Cyrus had abandoned the couch to prowl restlessly around the room, whereupon Sheng Ti had taken over his couch and was sound asleep; Ruthie nodded sleepily in her chair; Mr. Hitchens idly turned the pages of a magazine, and the tables were strewn with crumpled napkins and paper coffee cups.

Yet no one considered leaving; they remained

incapable of exchanging this place for their own quiet, empty rooms, knowing that if anything happened it would happen *here*. And what they were all waiting for, thought Robin sadly, was news that Mrs. Pollifax had been found. He did not think any of them were going to be rewarded for their vigil but he understood it; he had seen the hope in their faces each time the phone or radio signalled a message. Sleep was blurring their anxiety now — as he only wished it might blur his and Cyrus's — but the agonizing part for him about this long wait was the sense of helplessness. Somewhere in the Western district of Hong Kong Mrs. Pollifax was enduring this long night, too, surrounded by terrorists who were obviously not going to risk long radio transmissions or be found in any house-to-house search. They were up against that juggernaut that was moving slowly and inexorably toward conclusion, grinding down everyone in its path.

When the phone rang at half-past one, it was Robin who was nearest to it and who plucked it from its cradle. "Oh — yes, Your Excellency," he said, and at his words Cyrus stopped pacing, Marko turned from the radio to listen and Mr. Hitchens put down his magazine.

"No, nothing yet on our missing agent," Robin was saying. "Her husband's here, however — yes, her husband, it was he who thought of the Army. Now what about the Army, sir? Given the extreme need for secrecy on this—" He paused, listening, and his eyes brightened. "That's certainly good news, sir, the best we could hear but when—" He broke off, his face tightening and when he spoke again his voice was grim. "Not until then? That's your earliest guess? Yes, I understand it's the middle of the night but under the circumstances — no, the only information we have is that it will probably take place inside of the week but it's a very unreliable report, sir, mere conjecture as I reported to you earlier — yes, the housekeeper... All right, it does help the situation, sir, but of course a certain uneasiness remains as to... Yes, sir, I realize the situation. Very good, sir. Thank you."

He hung up and said flatly, "Tomorrow — midafternoon." With a glance at his watch he added, "That's thirteen and a half hours from now...He guarantees this can be put in motion by tomorrow, Friday, at 3 P.M., when details from the Army, in plainclothes, will begin patroling the Peak and the tower there, the power station, radio station and Government House on a round-the-clock basis."

"And why not sooner?" demanded Cyrus.

Robin said dryly, "He has reminded me that

terrorists inevitably time their attacks to co-incide with the prime-time evening news, so that they can get fullest coverage. He feels that bearing this in mind we needn't be too impatient about the delay that is necessary while he goes through proper channels. He also reminded me that it is almost two o'clock in the morning, that the Executive Council must be notified, and the soldiers briefed."

"Not good enough," Cyrus said flatly.

"No, my friend," said Marko, "but it is something. Please — sit down, you will wear yourself out, there are still possibilities."

At half-past two Duncan phoned with a report on the landlords of Dragon Alley, and Marko listened, scribbling furiously on a note pad. Turning to Cyrus and Robin he said, "This is the report on what property Charles Feng owns, all neatly concealed under company names, and, *mon Dieu* — just listen: under the name of Crystal Curio Enterprises the man owns half of Dragon Alley — numbers 31½, 30, and 28 — and there is your explanation of how he can somehow come and go without being seen. Under the title of Emperor Gems Limited he owns a warehouse, or *godown*, on the waterfront, and under the name of Green Jade Associates Limited there is a tailor shop. There may be more, his clerks are still searching..." Turning back to the telephone he said to Duncan, "Try the warehouse and the tailor shop – but carefully, my friend."

That was at half-past two. During the next hour there was only silence from both radio and telephone and they all waited at various levels of wakefulness, slumped in chairs or sprawled on couches.

It was at 4 A.M. that Cyrus suddenly stood up and said, "I've had enough of this!" He strode over to Sheng Ti. "Wake up, Sheng Ti," he said, shaking him, and as the young man sat up and rubbed his eyes Cyrus turned and said crisply, "Marko – call in your surveillants from Dragon Alley. Robin – wake up that third chap asleep in the bedroom... This feels too much like a wake to suit me, and it's the biggest damn waste of talent I've seen in years."

Marko said with a smile, "Taking over, are you, my friend?"

"Yes, damn it," Cyrus told him. "You may lose your jobs for this but the alternative for me could be losing my wife. This is what I suggest," he said, and then he shook his head and said flatly, "No, this is what we *do.*"

And quietly, but with firm authority, he told them very explicitly what could be done while they waited for channels to be gone through and the wheels of bureaucracy to turn.

# 16

# FRIDAY

There had been darkness, and then a dim small light. There had been a hook in the ceiling to which her bound wrists had been attached so that she hung suspended, just off the floor, while the man whose face she couldn't see asked questions, a great many questions, and then the nightmare had begun.

She hadn't dreamed it, had she?

She stirred, groaned and opened her eyes: something had changed, the dark room was gone and she was lying on the floor of a room that was brightly lighted, too brightly, it hurt her eyes and she closed them again, becoming aware now of searing hot flames running up and down her back and of something wet and sticky accompanying the tongues of flame. What was she doing here, she wondered, and where was she? There was too much for her to understand and she sank back into an oblivion that was part unconsciousness and part exhausted sleep.

When she opened her eyes again it was to the pain of remembering precisely where she was, and why: she was in Hong Kong, and she'd been questioned and then beaten so that she would submit and tell the faceless man what she knew; and why he hadn't killed her she didn't know, but that would probably happen next, and in her weakness she began to cry soundlessly, remembering that Cyrus was on his way to join her, and never to see him again — never see another morning, another spring, another summer...

Presently she grew angry at the waves of self-pity and grief and she thought crossly, *It's not that I expected clean sheets but that I resent very much ending my life on a filthy floor in a Hong Kong loft.*

That was better; anger was always better.

"So you're still alive," said a voice sardonically from somewhere beyond her view.

She opened her eyes and saw a foot nearby wearing a broken sandal, with a leg attached to the foot. Lacking the energy to lift her head and identify the voice it nevertheless reassured her: it was true, she *was* still alive, and now she remembered Eric the Red and being told by Alec Hao that the terrorist attack was planned for morning, and she wondered if it was morning yet. She told herself that it was time to stop feeling sorry for herself and learn what time it was. If she could lift her head. If she could move. If she could disentangle herself from the floor and sit up.

Resolutely she lifted her head, ignoring the ringing in her ears and the room beginning to spin, and she saw the wall she had originally occupied when she was brought here, and Detwiler somberly watching her. "Detwiler," she murmured, and the sound of her voice pleased and steadied her. She began to grow aware of sounds now: of voices, of footsteps hurrying back and forth, a laugh, and — what was that creaking noise in the background, so familiar yet odd, reminding her of clothes being hung on a clothesline? Ah yes, it was the sound of objects attached by ropes to a pulley. The window, she remembered now...Alec had said the windows could be lifted out, that there was a van parked in the alley below to which they lowered things. The plans were in motion, then, it was morning and the terrorists were on the move and if this was so then it was time for her to be on the move, too — *because*, she thought, *if you continue to lie here, Emily, they'll kill you, they certainly won't leave you behind.*

This thought startled her and she wondered where it had come from, and if it were true.

*But of course it's true,* said the small voice inside of her: *if you can't walk, can't even stand up, of what use are you to them? They certainly won't leave you behind* alive.

She wondered why it had occurred to her that she might go with them; did this small voice mean she might be used as a hostage?

*Why not,* replied this inner gadfly, adding somewhat tartly, *you might note that your back may be a bloody pulpy mess but they didn't touch your face, hands, legs or feet. Except for the blood running down your back you're still presentable.*

This galvanized her: she *must* sit up, then, and perhaps — who could predict? — she might next be capable of standing, and eventually be able to walk, too. Miracles could still occur and she would settle for a small one now. She drew several deep breaths, coughed, drew in several more and then with one reckless herculean movement rolled herself to the wall and pushed herself into the sitting position, biting back a scream of pain as her torn back met the wall. She had just lifted her bound wrists to look at her watch — it read 6:03 — when wave after wave of dizziness swept over her followed by nausea and then retching.

Sweating, weak, emptied, she resisted the longing to attach herself to the floor again, and waited.

Moments passed – hours – before she dared open her eyes again to discover that she felt steadier. Still, her situation was not very promising, she conceded, and now she began remembering what she had called *karate mind* in her classes with Lorvale Brown: the mobilizing of one's energy so that it could be directed to whatever part of the body one chose, usually the hand that would strike out with the speed and thrust of a bullet. She recalled the enormous concentration behind this, and the success of it, and she began to apply this formula now to her shaken body, resolutely summoning untapped reserves of strength to send to her arms, legs, feet. Illusion or not, it had an effect.

Beside her Detwiler said wearily, "It's all over now, you know, there's no hope, they're leaving any minute...by seven o'clock they'll have taken over the Peak."

She turned her head to look at him and met his eyes. He looked haggard and gray, and she wondered if Mrs. O'Malley would even recognize him now.

He said, "They made you talk?"

She thought back to the hell she'd gone through, not wanting to remember but feeling it was necessary for a moment. "No," she said. "I told them I loved the Buddha you gave me and decided I must keep it. I told them I'd seen a similar Buddha in the hotel gift shop and I thought you wouldn't notice the difference."

He looked startled. "You did that? You managed that? We could" — he moistened his lips with his tongue — "we could hear you scream — three times — and then your groans."

Had she screamed? She supposed that she must have.

"It was — terrible," he said, tears spilling from his eyes to run down his cheeks.

This was not at all helpful; she turned away and looked to her left, at Alec Hao, and discovered him so deeply asleep that the sounds and movements around them hadn't reached him at all. Her glance went beyond him to the window, which was wide open now, and to the cluster of men standing beside it looking down into the alley, calling out orders, gesturing; and then her gaze fell on the radio sitting on a crate some distance down the aisle from her, the radio on which a message had come through on what must have been another day.

Her eyes focused on it dreamily...a black box sitting on a wooden crate some seven feet behind the men at the window, whose backs were turned to it.

*Radio*...Marko had said, "For the radio-detection van there is a driver and the truck is a closed van, bristling with aerials inside, and once there is a signal..." and then, "at two and a half minutes they have gone beyond the safe limit...after two and a half minutes they are vulnerable to anyone who might wish to find them..."

Vulnerable to anyone who might wish to find them.

She thought, *If I could creep down this aisle to the radio I could flick on the transmitting switch. They wouldn't see me...not if I stayed low, crouched behind the crates...The only risky moment would come when I stand up to lean over and turn on the switch.*

If she could crawl...If she could stand.

She glanced down at her watch: it was six-fifteen and she might not have this much strength again; did she have *enough?*

Two and a half minutes was a long time, she noticed, seeing how slowly the second hand on her watch crept around the dial, but if the signal could last for two and a half minutes it would be heard and they could be traced and located.

"What is it?" asked Detwiler, seeing the

frown on her face.

She said softly, "The radio..."

"What about it?"

She turned her face toward him. "I've been thinking that if I could crawl over to it, and if the transmitters were turned on for two and a half minutes—"

He scowled, not understanding. "What would that do? Who would hear?"

She said simply, "It would be heard. A great deal has been happening, there are people — people hoping the radio may be used."

His eyes widened. "You mean — *others?* People *know?*"

"Yes — but not when," she told him. "Your papers — the plans you hid in the Buddha — are in good hands. So if I can get to the radio — I must ask, if the men should move away from the window could you possibly manage to create a diversion? The switch would have to — *must* — remain open for two and a half minutes."

He was silent, his face thoughtful, and she thought that for the first time since she'd come here he looked like the Detwiler she'd met on Monday.

"No," he said at last.

Her consternation, her sense of betrayal, were like a stab opening up wounds again. "You won't *help?*"

"No," he said softly, "I mean that I will go to the radio, not you." He turned to look at her. "You must — allow this." A curious little smile twisted his lips. "I've been of little use, and — I'm quite addicted, you know. Allow me to feel — be — a human being again."

"But—"

He touched her bound hands with his. "It's all right, you know — it's all right. It's the switch on the left side?"

She nodded. "Flip it on and come back." Something about him worried her. "Come back and we'll time it together."

He smiled faintly, nodded, and rolling himself to his knees he tipped forward and began to crawl awkwardly down the aisle. The men beyond were still occupied at the window, and when one did turn away to collect an additional box it was to another aisle that he went; Mr. Detwiler remained unseen.

As he came to a stop under the radio Mrs. Pollifax tensed: this was the dangerous moment, when he would have to struggle to his feet, stand upright and lean over the crate to flick on the switch. She waited, holding her breath. Pulling himself into a kneeling position Detwiler glanced back at her once and she saw that he was asking for a signal. Backs were still turned; she nodded vigorously, watched him place his weight on one leg, stand, lean over and push on the switch.

*"Beautiful – oh, you dear man,"* whispered Mrs. Pollifax, and drew an exultant breath of relief. As he sank back to the floor out of sight she lifted her tied hands to consult her watch and to mark the second hand: it was precisely six-twenty-nine...except – *Oh, God,* she thought, seeing how slowly the second hand moved, *it's going to take so long and how many times must the second hand crawl past the hour to two and a half minutes...150 times?*

*Four seconds,* she whispered, counting. *Five... eight...nine seconds...*

Detwiler was not returning. Snatching a quick glance at him she saw only his back as he crouched under the radio, but she could give him no more attention and her eyes fled back to the second hand's movements on her watch. *Fifty seconds...sixty...one minute!*

One minute and three seconds. One minute and five seconds...eight...nine...

How astonishing time was, she thought, how arduous just one second, did people *know* this?

One minute and fifty seconds...fifty-eight. Two minutes – the transmitter had been sending out its signal for two minutes.

Two minutes and one second...and now

Mrs. Pollifax allowed herself to hope...allowed herself to think of two men in a radio-detection van furiously turning those coordinates that Marko had described, their optimism mounting in tune with hers if only...if only...

Two minutes and twenty-seconds — please, please, she whispered; two minutes and twenty-five seconds ... twenty-six ... twenty-nine ... thirty seconds.

Two minutes and a half!

She felt a rush of joy and longed to call out to Detwiler that he'd done it, that the radio had remained on for two and a half minutes.

A sudden shout interrupted her vigil and she lifted her eyes from her watch. *"Oh no,"* she gasped, crying the words out loud as she saw the man standing over Detwiler and staring down at him in disbelief; she saw comprehension dawn on the man's face, saw the switch furiously snapped off and others come to stand over Detwiler, and then the gun drawn out of the gun belt.

She closed her eyes as they shot him. When she opened them Detwiler was dead, sprawled lifeless on the floor beside the crate, his eyes open and staring sightlessly down the aisle toward her.

# 17

Staring at Detwiler's body sprawled across the floor Mrs. Pollifax thought dazedly, *He knew this could happen, it's what he was trying to tell me, that he couldn't find a future for himself, there was no going back* . . .

*Poor Mrs. O'Malley,* she thought.

And then she remembered that it was an incredible act of gallantry on Detwiler's part, because it was she who had been going to crawl to the radio but he'd insisted on doing it instead, and at this she lifted her bound wrists to clumsily wipe away her tears.

Beside her Alec Hao suddenly sat up, jarred out of his sleep. "What is it?" he said sharply. "What's happened?"

She nodded toward Detwiler. "They've shot him."

He glanced down the aisle and then he turned to stare at her. "Is he dead? It's you I thought they'd killed, I didn't expect—"

"I know," she said.

Alec was shivering. "Are we next? Doesn't this ever end?"

She had watched the window being replaced and now she braced herself as Eric the Red strode down the aisle to the two of them and said curtly, "Up — on your feet, we're leaving."

She thought, *Well, Emily, this is when you find out what all those years of orange juice and vitamin pills can do for you...What you may want is a soft bed, hot food and a great deal of nurturing, but what you're stuck with is leaving this blessed wonderful floor and walking downstairs.*

It was Alec who helped her to her feet, which was generous of him, she thought, not realizing that as she'd leaned forward he'd seen her bloody back. Stumbling a little, she found that if she concentrated on Detwiler's final act of courage she could ignore the pain of her shirt tugging at her tender back. Step by step she followed Eric the Red down the stairs, and when she faltered Alec steadied her from behind.

The blue wooden door was open and she saw the van waiting in this other alley, the alley to which she'd been delivered by Mr. Feng an eternity ago. It was a surprisingly innocent-looking van, a shabby Volkswagen camper with what looked like baggage strapped on its roof and covered with a tarpaulin, and — *Oh what a clever touch*, she thought bitterly — two bicycles mounted at the back. Only the two rear windows were curtained, the others open to the world as if to emphasize there being nothing to hide, except that as she entered the van Mrs. Pollifax noticed what was hidden in the curtained rear: piles of machine guns, net bags through which could be seen tins of food, and crates marked AMMO.

But where was the radio-detection van?

She reminded herself that she was still alive and was apparently to be a hostage and to go on living a little longer — if no one grew nervous, if all went well — and now she applied herself to sitting down next to the uncurtained front window without her back touching the rear of the seat. But where was the radio-detection van?

Beside her Alec said softly, "Sunshine...I didn't think I'd ever see it again."

"No," she said, remembering that for him it had been three days. She looked carefully down at her wristwatch and saw that it was six fifty-five, or roughly twenty-three minutes since Detwiler's signal had been cut off, and she thought, *Surely this was time enough?* And then in a sudden panic she wondered if the men in the radio-detection van had stopped cruising the streets, had given up, or had perhaps taken a ten-minute break at half-past six. Detwiler had given his life for those two and a half minutes and she was appalled as she wondered if she had counted the seconds properly, if Marko had erred, if new equipment had been developed that protected these men against such a long radio signal.

She was shaken by these doubts and weakened from her walk down the stairs; the reserves of energy that she'd summoned were slipping away from her, and this too appalled her.

Others entered the van now, six men in all, and while Carl took the wheel the others arranged themselves out of sight in the rear. The van backed out of the alley and Mrs. Pollifax stared into narrow streets filled with people going to work, at barrows being wheeled along the crowded sidewalks, and two ancient men defying the streams of people by playing mah jong at a table under an awning: it was the beginning of Friday.

But she could see nothing on the street that resembled a radio-detection van, or for that matter any van at all.

Something had gone wrong, then — horribly and terribly wrong — and she felt the weight of it crush her spirit. She wondered if she could bear it. She had already exacted her last reserves of strength in walking down the stairs to the alley, and now her body was exacting its own price by supplanting hope with hopelessness; she realized that she had an overwhelming desire to cry.

From the back of the van came the sputtering of a radio and Eric the Red speaking in a low voice; she caught the words *coffee shop third floor,* and *take them to the top* and then, *about eight minutes now.* She realized that an advance party of terrorists must have already seized the tower and have found hostages. Hopeless, all of it – too late, too late...She closed her eyes to escape the unfeeling world outside and dreamily thought of home, of Mr. Lupalak, who might or might not have installed the bay window off-center, and then of Mr. Hitchens and his Learning Experiences; would he call this a Learning Experience?

When she opened her eyes they were on Peak Road, climbing now and moving at a moderate speed, a shabby camper with a woman at one window, bicycles mounted on the rear, luggage on the roof...the "luggage" that would be the multiple rocket launcher Robin had mentioned and that Mr. Hitchens had described, and for just a moment she gazed down at the harbor below and wondered what Robin and Marko were doing. *Sleeping, of course,* she thought, since it was scarcely 7 A.M., at which she felt acutely lonely and bereft.

The tower could be glimpsed now above the trees with its circular restaurant at the top that looked so much like a space capsule; the radio had gone silent and there was a feeling of mounting tension in the van. Her own tension was mounting, too, because once they reached the peak she would have to walk again, and she was remembering how casually these people killed.

Beside her Alec said weakly, "I can't stand it, this going on and on, not knowing – I don't think I can stand much more of it."

She realized that she could still be useful and comfort him, that there was sanity in doing this. With her bound hands she reached over and touched his arm. "I think," she whispered, and faltered. "I think," she said more resolutely, "that one *has* to go on – and on – and on."

Her words seemed to come to her from a great distance, echoing through caverns and valleys. Deep down she could feel the oppression of her own defeat, her own giving-upness, which was – she knew – compounded of the abuse her body had taken as well as sleeplessness, shock, hunger, the horror of Mr. Detwiler's death but worst of all his radio signal gone unheard. There was no longer anything she could do and now she was becoming incapable of feeling and even of thinking.

*Something's happening to my mind,* she thought, and found that she didn't care; if this were madness it at least promised a comfort that removed her from the reality she was meeting now. The van had drawn into the parking lot of the tower and its engine died. There were other cars parked there, the occupants hostage now, she supposed, and the grounds were deserted except for a solitary gardener, a young Chinese, patiently pruning rosebushes at a distance. She could hear the terrorists murmuring over the weapons they were collecting from the rear and then, "Out," said Carl, and she looked up to see him with a machine gun slung over one shoulder, grenades hanging from his belt and a pistol leveled at the two of them.

Drearily she arose, back in nightmare again, and she and Alec stumbled down from the van to begin the walk to the tower, the men behind them relaxed and chattering. An abrupt movement off to her left startled Mrs. Pollifax into lifting her head but it was only the gardener moving to another rosebush and dragging his sack behind him. She wanted to scream at him, *Fool — can't you see the guns, don't you realize all of Hong Kong's about to be taken hostage?*

But she remembered the world had its own way of going on and on, and there would always be gardeners trimming shrubbery and blind to catastrophe.

Except...except it was strange, she thought, how very closely the gardener had resembled Sheng Ti.

*I'm hallucinating now, of course,* she thought, *because Sheng Ti is down in the city and Sheng Ti is not a gardener*...Horrified at what was happening to her increasingly blurred mind, she looked away before the young gardener could turn into Robin or Marko, or even Cyrus.

They entered the tower, walking into a cheerless concrete hall, damp and cold from the night, with several shallow puddles of water lying on the floor. Dully she thought, *Abandon hope all ye who enter here*...The bank of elevators lay to their right and she stoically turned to the right, following the man in the lead. Ahead of them a man was standing in the hall waiting patiently for an elevator to arrive, and it did not surprise her at all that he looked exactly like Cyrus because this had to be what madness was like, this peopling the world with familiar faces.

This man-who-looked-like Cyrus regarded them all with interest, his gaze coming to rest at last on Mrs. Pollifax. "Good morning," this person said cheerfully. "Elevator's rather slow today."

"Oh?" said Eric the Red curtly.

His eyes were so kind, she thought — just like Cyrus's eyes — and his voice sounded so much like Cyrus's that tears came to her eyes. But Cyrus was a world away, he wasn't even in Hong Kong yet, was he? and she stared at him suspiciously, hating him for reminding her of Cyrus.

"Ah — coming down now," said this man who was impersonating Cyrus so deftly. "Some sort of army maneuvers?" he asked in a kindly voice, with a nod toward their weapons.

"Mmmm," grunted Carl.

Heads turned toward the arriving elevator but Mrs. Pollifax was stealing a second hungry glance at this man who looked like Cyrus. He had managed to move closer until he stood beside her, and she looked up at him wonderingly, turning away only when she heard the cage of the elevator jar to a halt at their floor.

She had assumed that she had gone beyond shock; she had assumed the elevator would be empty, she had assumed—

The doors opened and she screamed, confronted by an elevator crammed full of men and guns — Liberation 80's men cradling submachine guns pointed directly at them...it was to be a massacre after all, and this was the end...And then with a beautiful rush of sanity she saw the faces of Marko and Robin and Krugg and Upshot among the men in the elevator and understood at last: she had *not* been hallucinating, it had really been Sheng Ti outside, and it was truly Cyrus standing beside her now.

"Down, Emily!" shouted Cyrus, and, hurling himself at Mrs. Pollifax and Alec, he carried them both to the floor as the machine guns began spewing out their deadly fire.

# EPILOGUE

"Outwitted by a bunch of amateurs," Marko was saying with a smile and a shake of his head. "Interpol is incredulous and the Governor still somewhat in shock, amateurs having come to be regarded lately as relics from the Stone Age."

"Not in fashion at all," agreed Robin, and turning to Mrs. Pollifax he said, "It was Cyrus — entirely, Cyrus, you know. If it hadn't been for him—"

They were seated around a table in the Golden Lotus restaurant — where it had all begun, remembered Mrs. Pollifax, thinking back to Monday's breakfast with Mr. Hitchens, when he had pointed out the appearance of Lars Petterson to her; and now it was Friday evening and she was astonished at all that had happened in five days, and even more astonished at being alive and here at all.

Yet only partially here, she conceded, aware

that she still hovered between two worlds, the darker violent world holding her back from this one, whose language she had misplaced for the moment. Nevertheless she had insisted on being here, because at midnight Robin and Marko would be flying off to Rome, and as she had explained to Cyrus, the only alternative to sitting on a chair was to lie flat on her stomach, which was not only tiresome but boring.

"From what we've learned," said Marko quietly, "it would have been a terrible bloodbath. That position on the Peak is nearly impregnable: the government could have brought in helicopters, police, Army, Navy—" He shook his head. "At the slightest sign of activity the terrorists would have launched their rockets into the city below and killed crowds of innocent people. The terrorists could have held out for days, leveling whole sections of Hong Kong and leaving thousands homeless and dead."

Yes, that would have happened, she thought, nodding; she had no doubts about this because she had experienced — however briefly — the minds and the psyches of the men involved. As Marko knew, she thought, her eyes resting for a moment on his scarred face, and as Cyrus guessed, with his sensitivity so attuned to possibilities lurking behind the criminal mind.

For herself there had been X rays but she had refused to be hospitalized, wanting to stay with Cyrus. Instead she had placed herself in the capable hands of Dr. Chiang, who had biblically annointed her back with herbal and antibiotic salves, given her antitetanus injections, chicken broth and tea and a sedative, following which she had slept all afternoon. Her back would retain the scars of the beating for the rest of her life, he'd told her, but it was plain to him that, with her U.S. connections, she'd had value to them as a hostage or matters would have been much worse. He had then calmly described to her how much worse it could have been, naming the more sophisticated torture devices invented in this modern civilized world.

To this Mrs. Pollifax had listened attentively, wanting to learn what she would eventually be thankful for when the fires stopped raging up and down her back, and ultimately she had decided that yes, she had been very fortunate indeed.

The fires had now been reduced to smoldering embers, and six hours of sleep had restored her spirit so that she could say now, "Tell me — I want to hear all about it."

And waited, feeling rather like a child about to hear a wonderful story that might place her more firmly in this world she must reenter.

Robin smiled at her. "Yes . . . all right . . . but first you have to picture us sitting around in frustration in the small hours before dawn, napping and waiting for news of you, waiting for all the red tape to be cut before the Army could send in its men, except there was no news of you and it looked endless hours before the Army would be available, with this huge gap yawning between them and Friday afternoon when they'd take over.

"It was Cyrus who very suddenly stood up and announced around 4 A.M. that we were behaving like bloody fools, that we had five able-bodied men present in the room at that moment, plus Witkowski asleep in the bedroom, and Krugg and Upshot at their Dragon Alley posts, and there were Duncan's seven men from the special unit if Duncan could be sold on the idea of enthusiastic volunteers—"

"He refused the word volunteers," put in Mr. Hitchens.

"All right, amateurs," conceded Robin with a flash of a smile. "Amateurs like Cyrus and Mr. Hitchens and Sheng Ti and Ruthie who could help fill in those hours before the Army would arrive to do the job."

*This is very real to them,* thought Mrs. Pollifax, listening carefully and watching their faces, but realness still eluded her and the words came to her from a great distance.

Ruthie said cheerfully, "If I remember correctly, Cyrus pointed out that at least we'd feel we were *doing* something, and there was always the remote possibility that the Liberation 80's group might act sooner than anyone expected."

"As they certainly did," said Mr. Hitchens with feeling. "My God, when I think what would have happened if we'd not been there—" He received a warning glance from Ruthie and tactfully subsided.

"Mercifully, Duncan embraced the idea," continued Marko. "He didn't appreciate that twelve-hour gap, it worried him, too. In fact Duncan was ready to risk his job to contribute his seven men, but *only* if we agreed to go about it in a most professional manner, as if the Liberation 80's group might really strike."

Robin grinned. "Which none of us thought possible, of course. Except Cyrus."

Marko smiled back at him. "Yes, is that not startling? We gravely assured Duncan that we were most seriously intentioned and he gave us carte blanche and pledged himself and seven men. We conferred and decided we must concentrate our small group on the tower at the Peak, due to those two words *command post* inside Mrs. Pollifax's Buddha, so out into the cold, dark predawn we went."

Robin nodded. "We had Duncan's seven men posted in the top of the tower, fully armed—"

"The restaurant at the top doesn't open until noon, you see," put in Ruthie. "Only the coffee shop on the third floor was open."

"Yes," said Marko, smiling at her, "and Ruthie and Mr. Hitchens were given walkie-talkies and concealed beside the road behind shrubbery—"

"—with blankets and coffee," added Mr. Hitchens eagerly.

"—and with orders to report every vehicle that passed. Sheng Ti became a gardener outside, with a gun inside his sack—"

Sheng Ti beamed and nodded. "With a walkie-talkie, too. Not bad!"

Robin smiled. "But I must admit we were all of us — every one of us — completely shocked when we began to understand that terrorists were actually *arriving* and that this was to be the day. And the *hour*."

Sheng Ti said proudly, "I was first to see."

Ruthie nodded. "Yes, all Hitch and I did was report another car on its way to the Peak but it was Sheng Ti who watched two men park the car and leave it, carrying guns and heading for the coffee shop."

"Where eight people plus Krugg and Upshot were eating breakfast," pointed out Mr.

Hitchens. "All ten of them were herded together by the Liberation 80's men with machine guns — it must have been terrifying for those eight people — and taken up to the tower."

"Where we were waiting for them," said Cyrus, his eyes resting warmly on his wife. "Myself, Robin and Marko, that third Interpol chap, Whatsisname, and Duncan's seven men."

"It all happened so fast," breathed Mr. Hitchens.

"After which," added Marko, "there came the glorious news from Ruthie and Mr. Hitchens that a van was on its way to the Peak to join the advance party, and that Mrs. Pollifax had actually been seen at one of the windows."

Startled, Mrs. Pollifax realized that she was entering the story, and remembering back to that lonely, despairing ride up Peak Road she contrasted it with the triumphant scenario being described to her now and her sense of separateness from them all nearly overwhelmed her: she felt anchored in the estrangement that came from returning to life after an unsharable ordeal, and desperately aware, still, of those who had not returned and who never could. And then two things happened: across the table she met Alec Hao's gaze and saw the same grief in his eyes and shared it with him, smiling at him reassuringly; and sensing her withdrawal from them all Cyrus reached for her hand and pressed it.

And suddenly the darkness lifted from her and she experienced the miracle of feeling again. Of being connected...to herself...to life...to Cyrus...to Alec...to these warm and wonderful people. It was like stepping out of a tomb to be met with sunlight and a flood of tenderness.

"So Cyrus came down to ground level," Robin explained. "To wait for you, hoping that his standing so innocently by the elevators would alert you to the fact that something was going to happen."

"Not wishing," pointed out Marko, "to lose you in the crossfire."

Mrs. Pollifax smiled ruefully as she remembered, grateful to be entering their story willingly now. "I thought — I really believed I was hallucinating," she told them. "That it couldn't possibly be Sheng Ti outside pruning rosebushes, and as for Cyrus already in Hong Kong and waiting for an elevator at the tower, of all places! I had to have gone mad."

"But you were in shock," Ruthie reminded her. "As Dr. Chiang pointed out...From being beaten," she added gently. "From seeing Mr. Detwiler killed."

*From being beaten, from seeing Detwiler killed...*

Mrs. Pollifax thought that someday, perhaps on a summer's day among her flowers, she would allow it all to come back to her and she would try to make sense out of a world that could produce trips to the moon and silicon chips and computer robots and satellites, yet never touch the impoverished hearts that could still torture, terrorize and kill without mercy or feeling. But not now, not yet.

She would think about Detwiler instead: Detwiler, who had been abused and tricked and manipulated, and who had fluctuated between weakness and strength, vanity and sacrifice, until he had determined at last to assert himself and to act, even to die rather than to submit any longer...yes, she must remember Detwiler instead just now.

She saw that they were all staring at her, anxious and wondering. "I was thinking of Mr. Detwiler," she explained. "When he sacrificed himself to turn on the radio signal it wasn't entirely in vain, was it?"

Marko shook his head. "No, my dear Mrs. P., not entirely. In fact if it had not been for Cyrus, rallying us all in our most discouraged moment, Mr. Detwiler's act could have been all that might have saved you and Alec. The signal was heard and the building found. The three men in the radio van had to call for reinforcements, at which time Duncan told them that two terrorists had already arrived at the tower and that the situation was so far under control. They were instructed to follow you in a car to the Peak, keeping their distance. No — Detwiler's act was not wasted."

Mrs. Pollifax's glance went to Alec Hao. "You can perhaps forgive him now?"

"Forgive but not forget," Alec said in a hard voice. "At least he didn't actually kill my father, it's Mr. Feng who — who—" His voice broke.

Marko said curtly, "Feng's dead, he shot himself after being questioned."

Alec said, "Then for God's sake tell me what was behind all this hell he created!"

Marko sighed. "Once the terrorists had taken over Hong Kong they were to demand — Feng's words — that all talks between Peking and Great Britain be suspended until the Nationalist Chinese on Taiwan could be included in the 1997 restoration of Hong Kong to China."

"Was the man insane?" exploded Alec.

Marko's voice was dry. "All fanatics are more or less insane, I suppose. He'd been working for years to undermine Communist China and — failing that — he was determined to prevent Hong Kong being given to them. He spoke of years of planning," said Marko. "The acquiring of property in different sections of Hong Kong where arms and ammunition could be hidden away — we think there must have been help from his brother and other sympathizers in Taiwan on this — and then the first contact with the Liberation 80's group through his nephew Xian Pi, followed by the theft of diamonds to finance the operation, and then the methodical distribution of those diamonds to buy guns and silence, bribes everywhere to close the eyes and ears of men."

*And to subjugate Mr. Detwiler,* thought Mrs. Pollifax.

"But in the end," Marko added sadly, "I think his motives were reduced to the same motives as the Liberation 80's group: he wanted to bring Hong Kong down in ruins and to express his hate and rage to the world. He must have known it was too late, that his dream of a Nationalist government returning to mainland China was impossible, but he'd given his entire life to the scheme, and he believed Taiwan to still be the true government of China."

Robin broke in to say, "That was Feng's passion, but the Liberation 80's group, on the other hand, were going to demand ten million in gold for themselves and safe passage out of Hong Kong, probably to Libya."

Mrs. Pollifax shook her head over the madness of it all. "And Eric the Red?"

"Dead," Robin told her without expression. "He and two others were killed at the elevator. The remaining terrorists have been showing the police where the random bombs were planted — rather a lot of them, too," he added, "thereby hoping for reduced prison sentences, which is highly unlikely. Rumors are running high in Hong Kong, but the Governor's suppressed all news about this until the last bombs have been found. To avoid panic."

"But of course," said Marko quietly, "the main purpose of the Liberation 80's group — and the reason they were open to Mr. Feng's diabolical scheme — was the sense of power they'd achieve. Still another strike against law and order and civilizing governments — and undoubtedly a sense of renewal at being in action again, at sitting up in the tower with their guns and hostages and looking down at the rest of us with contempt."

There was silence and then Cyrus said, "But it didn't happen."

"Not this time, no," said Marko. "Not here, not now, not this time."

They reflected on these words until Mr. Hitchens lifted his glass of champagne and said, "Then I suggest we drink a toast to what didn't happen, and perhaps Mrs. Pollifax would care to add something to that?"

She smiled at him. "Yes — yes I think I'd like to," she said, and thought about this while her gaze moved from one person to the next at the table around her: to Marko with his wise-old-soul eyes, to Robin with whom she'd shared a second adventure, to Sheng Ti who would soon enter the United States with Lotus — Carstairs had assured her of this only an hour ago — and to Alec Hao who had lost a father but regained a future.

Her glance moved to Mr. Hitchens, diligently collecting his Learning Experiences, and to Ruthie, who had apparently collected *him*... She thought too of the cable she'd received only an hour ago from Bishop: DON'T EVER EVER DO THIS TO US AGAIN STOP CARSTAIRS APPLYING ICE PACKS AND TAKING SEDATIVES STOP CABLE ARRIVAL TIME NEW YORK AND WARN CYRUS OF LARGE AF-FECTIONATE DEMONSTRATIONS TO THANK FOR RESCUING STOP ALL LOVE BISHOP.

Her eyes met Cyrus's last of all — Cyrus, with whom she was to continue living after all, savoring those small exquisite joys of sharing.

Lifting her glass she gave him a radiant smile and said with feeling, "To amateurs — angry, determined, caring amateurs...And to what almost — but didn't — happen in Hong Kong."

35-6
86
n2-3
222-3
228
287
113
240
289

17
6"
12"
15"

76.5        76  12

8    93.5   = 104
            - 94
            10"

P